BoX

BoX

Lucas Heath

ISBN 13: 978-0-9989827-1-7

Acknowledgments

A huge thank you goes to some of the best people in my life, Brock, Todd, Jake, Stefan, and Ben, for their support and encouragement, not only in my writing, but my life.

Another thank you goes to Bev, who has undoubtedly helped increase the quality of my writing and stories.

Contents

Erased

1: Marsha and Barry

The room was a cube. It was twenty feet in height, length, and width, and the walls seemed to glow a stunning white that surpassed the purity of fresh-fallen snow. There were no windows, no doors, and no blemishes of any kind, just solid walls that boxed the young girl inside with no way of escape.

Her fragile body lay sprawled upon the solid white ground, shaking from cold. Fear had yet to settle in, for she had not yet awakened.

As time ticked away, her eyes opened and her head jerked up from the floor of her prison. Her head pivoted and tilted as she surveyed her surroundings. The beat of her heart quickened as she realized her predicament.

She remembered her identity, and where she was from, though why she was in this strange place escaped her memory. She sat up and grabbed at her neck, letting trembling fingers glide across the soft, tan skin. A bump where somebody had stuck a needle, found its place underneath her index finger and she rubbed at the spot, ignoring the pain. Someone had drugged her though the reason as to why eluded her.

Panic threatened to overtake her mind. The fight-or-flight instinct gripped at her heart, but with a deep breath she pushed the feelings away. Her father had always said,

Lucas Heath

"Marsha, fear is an illusion that makes you weak. You either learn to control it, or it will control you." She agreed with that statement and made destroying fear in her life a goal.

Marsha stood and felt her legs wobbling underneath her. Using the wall for support, she steadied herself and took another deep breath, letting it out at slow pace. A pedestal in the center of the room drew her attention. Sitting atop the square stand was a single pistol, though she didn't know what kind it was, or if it had ammunition.

Deciding to avoid the death device, Marsha turned toward a wall and ran her hands over it. It was smooth like marble and radiated a luminescent light that gave the room its glow. If it weren't for these walls, floor, and ceiling, darkness would reign. She followed the wall around the entire cube, feeling for any switches or hidden panels, though she found nothing.

After a final pass, Marsha leaned against and slid down a wall until her bottom hit the ground. She rested her head against her knees and cried.

****

Barry had a different reaction to his predicament, which began with a panic attack and then a surge of rage. He was alone, trapped in a glowing white cube with no food or water. He spent an hour kicking and slamming his fists against the walls, but left no sign he had done so. They were solid and seemed unbreakable. He had tried grabbing the gun from the pedestal in the center of the room, but a strong surge of electricity knocked him off his feet the moment he touched it. He wept and fumed as he stomped around the room, trying to figure out what he could do to change his circumstances.

"I don't deserve this!" He ranted for a while, though he wasn't sure if anyone was even listening. Someone *had* to be listening, right? They wouldn't just lock him up and leave him be, would they? Who were *they*? Why take *him*? Barry was a waiter at a small restaurant in Buffalo, New York. Why was *he* so special?

He sat and looked at the clothing he was wearing. Someone had changed him while he was unconscious. He wore gray sweatpants, a gray sweatshirt with his name embroidered on the left side of the chest, and he was barefoot. Allowing him to have socks and underwear would be too much of a luxury.

What if he had to go to the bathroom? There weren't any toilets or sinks, or even a bucket. How would he get food? The walls were solid and left no indication they could contain a door. There weren't even any vents in the room so the thought of running out of air made him calm and breathe at a steady pace. He stared for a while at the bloody knuckles he had gotten from punching a wall and wiped them against the leg of his sweatpants.

Something had to happen soon, and he would have to wait until that moment came.

2: Chuck and Elisa

The room was silent as her eyes fluttered open. She stared at the glowing white ceiling of the cube and a smile formed at the corners of her mouth; she had committed suicide and was now in Heaven. Sitting up, her head pounded to its own beat. The light added to her headache. She looked down at the black cross tattooed onto the back of her dark brown hand. Even from looking upside down, she could see her name, Elisa, embroidered into the gray sweatshirt she now wore. Wasn't she supposed to get a new body?

Elisa stood and gazed around the room with a look of confusion displayed on her face. Could she be in a holding room before seeing God? That didn't sound right. The glowing walls seemed to dim as if answering her mental plea for less light. In the center of the room rose a pedestal with a gun resting on top. She walked over and studied it.

"Where am I?" The words escaped her mouth in a British accent and echoed as though she were in a cave or tunnel. "This can't be hell, can it? It's too beautiful." She dismissed the gun and walked around the room, looking for any clues that would define her reality.

Elisa's mind raced at the possibilities of her location. Perhaps aliens had abducted her after taking the pills. No, that idea was absurd. Maybe someone had found her dying and called for help. Perhaps they had locked her in a mental hospital though that wouldn't explain the gun in the center of the room *and* the walls would have thick padding.

"Hello, can anyone hear me?" She called out as she looked toward the ceiling corners, hoping to see a camera watching her. "Hello?" The thick accent filled the room once more and Elisa sat cross-legged on the cold, glowing floor. Perhaps she needed to wait for an angel to come get her. She leaned up against a wall and closed her eyes. Other than her breathing and the pounding of her head, there were no noises coming from anywhere, as though the strange cube was soundproof. She expected to at least hear harps playing.

Another possibility nagged at her. Perhaps the pills put her in a coma and this was just a dream. That theory seemed more probable considering her situation didn't match up to what she had grown up learning in church. She didn't feel depressed anymore, that much was obvious, and she enjoyed the mental freedom. Perhaps the cube represented her brain, and she was trapped inside a coma. No matter the answer, as long as she wouldn't have to face the outside world, she felt at peace with where she was.

****

The moment Chuck awoke, he jumped to his feet and spun around to study his prison. "Four walls, one floor, one ceiling, estimated between fifteen and twenty feet. It's a cube," he said to himself as he took frantic mental notes. "Light emits from every direction preventing shadows. A single pistol rests on a podium in the center of the room." He walked over to the gun and reached down to touch it. He yanked his hand back the moment he felt and saw the hairs on the back of his hand stand on end. "Electrified; interesting," he mumbled. He ran a hand through his thick, black hair and circled the pedestal.

He moved over to one wall and knocked on it. "Solid, yet smooth, but not stone, possibly glass," he continued to mutter. "Though I'm sure it's unbreakable," he added as if he were trying to convince himself of that idea.

Chuck closed his eyes to recall what had happened. He had been sitting on a train, traveling from Mississippi to New Jersey, when a sharp pain shot through his neck and he awoke in the cube.

He reached for the right side of his neck and found the bump he had been expecting. "Sedative," he confirmed with a nod to himself and sat. "I know who you are," he called out as he looked around the cube. "I know what you're doing." He waited in silence. "I promise that I will stop you. You didn't win last time and you *won't* win this time." A grin appeared on Chuck's face and he stared at the gun. He already knew he was a lab rat in an experiment and he would not lose.

The light in the room increased, causing Chuck to shield his eyes while they adjusted. A voice echoed throughout the room as if it were coming from every direction.

BoX

"Participants, we selected you at random for this upcoming experiment." The deep gravel voice was that of an older man; it sounded as though the announcer had smoked most of his life. "My name is Jacob Harding and I would like to welcome you to The Box."

3: The Experiment: Tommy

A young boy nearing the age of fourteen stood by the pedestal in his cube and stared at the strange, black gun. His body shook with fear and tears dripped down his face. Nothing made sense to him anymore. He had been at school and was about to return to class from recess when he blacked out. Now, he was ... well ... only God knew where he was.

He looked down at the new clothing he wore. Gray sweatpants covered the recent scars from surgery on his thigh. A gray sweatshirt with his name, Tommy, stitched above his heart, covered his bruised torso. He wasn't wearing any shoes, socks, or underwear, which disturbed him. Even with the two materials of clothing, he felt naked and vulnerable.

The light from the surrounding walls pulsated with a rhythmic intensity. First, they would dim and then grow brighter. It was quite soothing and caused his body to stop trembling, and at any other time Tommy may have enjoyed it, but the tears kept falling down his cheeks. He wanted his dad. He made his way over to a corner, curled up into a ball, and sobbed.

Tommy wasn't sure if he had fallen asleep, or even how much time had passed, and without warning the light in the cube strengthened and a voice filled the room.

BoX

"Participants, we selected you at random for this upcoming experiment My name is Jacob Harding and I would like to welcome you to The Box."

Tommy sat up and searched for the source of the voice. There were no signs of a speaker anywhere in the room.

"This experiment has one simple rule. Be one of the twenty-seven individuals to make it out alive and you will be free to return to your homes."

By the rough voice of the man, he seemed old to Tommy, though the words being spoken were not falling on deaf ears. He was listening to find out how he could get back to his parents.

"How far will you go to save yourself? We have taken each one of you from varied walks of life. We have a vigilante, a Christian, a Hindu, a lawyer, a doctor, a teenager, a mother, and on goes the list. Like I said, there are twenty-seven of you and several tests. It is possible that many of you could survive, but knowing human nature as I do, I can guarantee that almost none of you won't."

Tommy shook again. He could die here?

"Now, let's begin, shall we?" There was a laugh from Jacob Harding and he cleared his throat before continuing. "You are all enclosed within your own personal cube. However, each room makes up an even larger cube I like to call The Box. Three cubes high, wide, and long. Think of it as a Rubik's Cube. Each cube has its own number designated to it from one to twenty-seven, though you will not know which number belongs to whom."

Tommy bit one of his fingernails. It was a nervous habit his parents had tried getting him to break, but now it was the furthest thing from his mind. He needed to survive.

"We will explain each test as they happen, so I won't go into details right now. You may have noticed the gun in the center of your cube. The electricity guarding it has deactivated, making it available for use. If at any point you decide that you would rather not take part in a test, you have one bullet to end your life. In doing so, the current test will end for everyone else. It's possible that your suicide could save the lives of several others."

Tommy stood and walked over to the gun. He reached out and picked it up, turning it around in his hands. His mom hated guns and his dad would have grounded him for life if he knew his son was holding one. Would Tommy ever be able to pull the trigger on himself? He doubted it, but then again, he did not understand what kinds of tests they would conduct on him.

"First, before we begin a test, I want to give you all a little treat. You may select one wall in your cube to make transparent for a brief period. This includes the floor *and* ceiling if you can somehow make it up there. Make your choice by placing your hand on the desired surface."

BoX

Tommy replaced the gun and looked at the five options surrounding him. He turned to the one behind him and walked over to it. With hesitation he placed his hand against the glowing wall. Sunlight replaced the artificial light, and he had to shield his eyes from the warming rays. The barrier was still there, but he was looking upon a vast, green field from up high. For the first time since he awoke, a small smile crept upon his lips. He was at the top of this Box.

The view vanished as fast as it had appeared, being replaced by the familiar glowing partition. Without thinking too much about it, he ran to grab the gun and set it next to the wall he had just touched. He needed to remember which direction led to the field. Perhaps it would help him later.

"Well then, I suppose that's all for now. The first test will begin tomorrow. Get some sleep!"

The lights in the cube faded, leaving Tommy in darkness.

4: Test One: Shelly and Barry

Shelly sat in darkness, her mind numb from the isolation. She didn't know how much time passed though it felt like hours. She mumbled inaudible sentences as the walls of the cube pressed up against her mind.

Before the lights went out, she saw a man when she touched a wall, making it transparent. The name written across his shirt was Barry. He was near her, but had his hand pressed up against the floor, seeing everything beneath him. When the floor became clear, it looked like he would fall right through, though he appeared to float on air.

He couldn't see Shelly watching him. The wall must have acted as a one-way mirror, allowing only her to see him when placing her hand against the glass.

Her sanity diminished when darkness consumed her. She wanted to stay strong, and she hoped to be free and see her family again, but she already knew there was no chance of her survival. A weight of hopelessness settled on her shoulders as though someone had slipped a pack of bricks upon her back.

Her family ... her students ... what would they do without her? The questions nagged on in her mind. Being a teacher was her life. It was something Shelly always wanted to be. She had never gotten married, nor had kids of her own, but it didn't matter. She was helping a young generation succeed, to be all they could be for the country, or what remained of it.

A glow appeared in the cube as though the lights were warming up and increasing in brightness. After a few minutes, the walls and ceiling were back to their original color of stunning white. The floor, however, remained black as night. Shelly noticed that the pedestal no longer existed, and the gun was lying on the floor.

"Welcome to test number one." The voice was not Harding's; this one was female. "The ground below you will soon decrease in temperature and simulate walking on dry ice. Skin that touches the floor can freeze and cause instant frostbite. This test will continue for one hour, or until someone ends their life. Let's see if human preservation wins out."

Shelly's mind kicked into gear as she heard the woman's final words. "You people are evil!" she screamed out, hearing her voice echo back to her. "You're putting us through hell! Do you hear me? You're putting us through hell!" She looked down at her bare feet and now understood why the people who ran this twisted experiment didn't want their test subjects wearing shoes. She could already feel the ground cooling.

Shelly had to survive, didn't she? She couldn't lose, not yet. She had to at least *try* to stay alive. Stripping off her sweatshirt and pants, she exposed her slender, naked body. She bunched them up together in the corner of her cube, and after grabbing the gun from the center of the room, stood on the clothing pile. The surrounding air cooled, and she shivered. She was thankful that her feet were small and needed little room to stand. She could only hope the hour would pass by with speed.

****

Several vulgar words escaped Barry's mouth as he tried to figure out what he should do. "I'm Governor Dane's son! You can't do this!" He jerked his head back and forth, looking around for any way of escape. He thought about removing his clothing to protect his feet, but without underwear, and with the possibility of these perverts watching, he didn't want to give them the satisfaction.

When the cold became almost unbearable, he removed his shirt and wrapped it around both feet, though without more layers the cold seeped through the fabric. He cursed many times before removing his pants and adding more protection underneath him. He eyed the gun a few steps away. There was no way he would use the weapon on himself, but he would love to use it on the man who put him in the cube.

"At least answer me this question!" He called out. "You've got me standing here naked. I deserve at least *some* explanation!" The air in the room seemed to change, and he took deeper breaths. "Why did you choose me? What did I ever do that made me a target for you sick freaks?"

BoX

He waited for several minutes, but without a response. "Tell me!" he screamed at the top of his lungs. Spittle flew from his mouth and froze the moment it touched the ground.

"You *know* why we chose you," the woman who had announced the test answered. "We took people from all walks of life, with all kinds of different morals. Sure enough, we *will* test those."

"But I'm just the son of a governor!" Barry spat. "I'm nobody special!"

"Barry, we didn't take you because you're a governor's son, or because you're a waiter at a restaurant." Her voice sounded eerily sweet, almost like a mother talking to her child. "We took you because you're a killer."

A chill spread through Barry's body, though it wasn't because of the floor. "But, how...?"

"Now, no more questions. Finish the test or take your life. It's your choice."

5: The Conversation: Tommy and Levi

By the time the test had finished, twenty-seven, shivering, naked victims had pressed themselves against the glowing walls of their cubes, standing on a small pile of clothing. Several of them had lost layers of skin from their feet, but everyone had escaped any real harm. The floor returned to its normal, white glow as the temperature increased.

"The test has ended. You may now clothe yourselves," the announcement came over the invisible intercom. The woman's voice sounded kind, a change from when she first announced the test. "Nobody has failed. Each one of you has figured out a way to avoid touching the ground, but at the cost of your dignity. As a reward, one wall in your cube will become transparent, giving you the opportunity to communicate with another individual."

Tommy poked the floor with his pinky finger to make sure it had returned to normal. Satisfied with the results, he slipped his chilled clothing back on, hiding his bruised skin.

After several minutes, the wall opposite Tommy's gun vanished, revealing an older gentleman the boy guessed was in his forties. He sat in the center of his cube and turned toward Tommy when he saw which wall had gone transparent.

BoX

Tommy approached the now open space with caution and reached his hand toward where the wall had been. He felt the barrier though he couldn't see it.

"Tommy, eh?" The older gentleman asked with tender warmth that surprised the young boy. He had a southern twang in his voice. "My father's name was Thomas."

Tommy sat at the edge of his cube and saw the name stitched into the man's sweatshirt. "Hello, Mister Levi, sir."

The man laughed and shook his head. "Just call me Levi. Everyone does. Well, when I'm not at work, anyway."

Tommy just stared at the man, for he wasn't sure what to say. He never talked with other adults, which was a rule his parents had given him.

"I can't believe they brought children into this twisted place," Levi muttered and shook his head. "I'm the one supposed to uphold the law and protect the citizens, and I couldn't even stop them from kidnapping us."

"You're a cop?" Tommy asked.

Levi nodded. "I am, though it looks like you've stripped me of that identity in here."

Tommy's body quivered, and he slid himself backward. His dad had always told him that police were the enemy of the people. They kept order and imposed insane laws for the sake of control.

"Son, are you all right?" Levi asked, noticing the boy's hesitation and sudden shift in mannerisms.

Tommy shook his head and stopped when he was in the center of his cube. "I'm not supposed to talk to people like you," he said. He knew he could get away with holding a gun, but if his dad found out he had been talking with a cop, he would never see daylight again.

Levi nodded. "I can understand that. The police aren't popular these days, but considering your situation, you can make an exception."

Tommy shook his head. "No, I can't. My dad would *kill* me if he found out I was talking to you." He looked up toward the ceiling, hoping that someone was watching him. "Please put the wall back!" He called out.

"Son, please. Talk with me." Levi stood and walked to the invisible, but present partition.

"Return it, please!" Tommy begged as he scooted backward. His back hit the wall leading to the field. He could see the older man staring at him, his eyes wide with disbelief and confusion. The opacity appeared once again isolating Tommy in the cube.

The young boy cried as his hand slid over the recent scar on his thigh. He nestled his head between his knees and let the tears flow. No matter how much he tried to convince himself otherwise, he didn't want to be with his father or mother. He wanted to stay as far away from them as possible. "Please, don't send me back home," he pleaded, though it wasn't directed toward anyone in particular. "Please, don't send me home."

6: Food: Chuck and Marsha

It was after his conversation with a woman named Diana that the lights in the cube ceased to glow, bathing Chuck in darkness. This twisted experiment was even crueler than the last one he experienced. Both times it had been against his will, but the first time he didn't have his memory to help him.

He tried finding a comfortable position to sleep in though it seemed impossible. The ground was as hard as marble, which made sleeping difficult. Exhaustion soon won out, and he drifted into a fitful slumber.

It was the nightmares that woke him and not the light of the cube. Demons from the past wove their way into every image that flashed through his dreams.

"Oh, come on, Chucky boy. You will not shoot me." An older man growled as Chuck placed the barrel of a revolver against his chest.

"I'm sorry, dad," Chuck replied. "I can't let this madness continue." He pulled the trigger of the gun and awoke with a jerk. Teardrops escaped his eyes and fell to the floor as images from the dream haunted him. He wiped his cheeks dry with a sleeve and noticed that the pedestal was back in the center of the cube.

BoX

Chuck stood and stretched his aching muscles though it didn't seem to lessen the pain *or* the kink in his neck. He salivated when he saw the tray of food on the square stand.

"Eat up, kids," Jacob Harding's voice echoed. "Your next test will soon begin, and for some of you, it will be your last meal."

Chuck hadn't realized how hungry he had gotten over the past, well, however many hours had passed since he had eaten food. Time in The Box was relative. The creators were the ones who controlled the sleep cycles, which he could tell were quite skewed. Grapes, a small chicken drumstick, and a glass of orange juice filled his belly within minutes.

Satisfied with the amount of food now sustaining him, he looked around at the glowing walls and sighed. They brought him into the room somehow. A hidden door had to be *somewhere*. He needed to continue searching though he only had until the next test began. He left the tray on the pedestal and looked.

****

"Marsha, you need to stop fearing this situation." Her father stood in front of her as she gawked at his sudden appearance. "You own this place, girl! Snap out of it! Give 'em hell! They don't control you, you manipulate *them*. As long as they think they own you, they can make you do what they want. Show them that my baby girl won't be owned by nobody!"

Lucas Heath

Marsha awoke as the lights in the cube glowed once more, brightening up the area. Her dad was even entering her dreams now, which to her, was a disconcerting reality. It's not that she didn't love her parents, she did, but they had a way of always sticking their nose in her business when she wanted to figure things out on her own. They gave great advice, but for once, she wanted to be independent.

The initial fear of being tested on had dispersed within the first few hours of Jacob's announcement. She had passed the first test without a problem and got to speak with a handsome young man named Elijah. He let her do all the talking and only interjecting once or twice in agreement to what she was saying. If the circumstances had been different, she would have asked him to dinner.

Marsha's dreams faded from her mind as she yawned and opened her eyes. The stand in the middle of the room had returned and something was on it. It wasn't until she stood that she could see what was there.

"Food!" She charged for the clump of grapes and devoured them. She tore into the meat and gulped down the orange juice.

"Eat up, kids. Your next test will soon begin, and for some of you, it will be your last meal."

The words barely reached Marsha's ears as she swallowed another bite of chicken and finished the juice.

When no more food remained, she sat and leaned against the pedestal, letting the contents of her stomach settle.

"You own this place, girl! Snap out of it! Give 'em hell!" her father's words from the dream flashed through her mind. It was a good suggestion, but how could Marsha accomplish that? Jacob Harding had all the power and could eliminate her whenever he wanted.

Marsha took a deep breath and pushed a sudden surge of panic away. She could at least follow one of her father's suggestions, which was to avoid letting these people fill her with fear. For the other stuff though, she would have to figure it out herself.

7: Test Two: Elijah

Elijah's head still spun from all the information Marsha had released. He hadn't fallen asleep, but sat in darkness, thinking about the poor girl he had met. She was a city girl though she lived in the suburbs. She had owned a cat named Cocoa though Cocoa died after being bitten by a venomous spider. Marsha had searched for true love and almost got married, though only two days before her wedding, found out her fiancé had cheated on her. The list continued on and Elijah had to admit that it made his problems seem less significant.

The lights had only been off for about an hour before turning back on again. "Well, that's a way to screw with everybody's sleep patterns," he muttered as he stood and stretched his legs. Somehow, someone had replaced the pedestal *and* given him food in the dark without making a sound, which was unsettling. He ate the food, savoring every bite.

After a short time, the female announcer's voice reverberated around the room. The first time Elijah heard her, she had seemed familiar somehow, though he couldn't place it. Now was no different.

"Test two is about to begin. Please stand."

Elijah obeyed. He looked around, wondering what would happen next.

BoX

"As mentioned before, each one of your cubes has a number from one to twenty-seven. You will all be voting for the purging of three cubes."

"Purging? You want *us* to decide who should die?" Elijah asked in disbelief.

"Call out a number between one and twenty-seven. We will tally the results and the inhabitants of the top three chosen cubes will die. Other than the number, you won't know who you are voting for and you may even select yourself as a target."

Elijah fell to his knees and tears filled his eyes. How could he take part in something so barbaric? "What if I don't want to choose?" He asked aloud, hoping she would hear him.

"Not selecting a number is a vote for yourself. Votes are now being accepted."

Elijah shook his head. "I won't choose a number. Who are *you* to ask me to do such a thing?" He stood and looked around the room. "You're not God! I know God and you *aren't* Him." He let the tears flow as he spoke, not bothering to wipe them away. "I don't care what kind of data you are recording from this experiment. You are forcing innocent people to take the lives of others! Just end this now, I beg you. Just end it now!"

Lucas Heath

"Poor, ignorant Elijah," the woman responded. Her voice had become cold. "*Nobody* is innocent. In this group of twenty-seven people alone, we have a murderer, a terrorist, a rapist, a dirty cop, a vigilante, a whore, a child abuser, and a lawyer who gets these kinds of people out of jail. Need I say more? You may have your cute, Christian values, but they count for nothing."

"Are you saying these people don't deserve a second chance? That they don't deserve love? You're not even giving them justice!"

"This *is* justice. Justice is just a group of individuals deciding the fate of another for their mistakes."

"So everyone in The Box deserves death? The teenager you mentioned earlier deserves to die? *I* deserve to die? What have I done that makes you think I am worthy of death? What makes me guilty?"

"Elijah," the tone of the woman's voice dropped. "Who do you think came up with The Box?"

In an instant, the tears dried up and a look of pure horror flashed across Elijah's face. "Oh, God, no," he whispered. "But, how could you," he paused as he understood. "You're Doctor Barbra Jenkins." His eyes grew wide, and the tears returned.

BoX

"Those twisted ideas you came up with were helpful, Elijah. I can say with no hesitation I am happy I was your psychiatrist."

"But that was years ago, when I was a teenager! I never meant for what I said to become a reality!" He fell to his knees and covered his face with his hands.

"Don't you know what your bible says? Life and death are in the power of the tongue, and those who indulge in it shall eat of its fruit. This is just the fruit of what you spoke. Now, are you going to select a number, or not?"

For the longest time, Elijah couldn't reply, but after reaching for something by the pedestal, he pushed himself to his feet. "No, I'm not," he said as he lifted the pistol to his head. "I'm not doing this to escape, but to save the others. I won't be the one responsible for their deaths. God, forgive me." He pulled the trigger.

An ear-piercing gunshot filled the room, and the light went out, leaving the cube in darkness.

8: Bathroom: Elisa and Barry

Twenty-six cube members waited for several minutes to hear the results of the tally. Most of them hoped the number they chose wouldn't add to someone else's tally, for they didn't want the guilt of being the reason another individual died. Some opted to choose themselves, risking their own lives instead of betraying their morals. After an agonizing wait, the voice of Barbra Jenkins filled the room. Elisa listened with attention. She had picked the number zero, which meant she had selected herself. Perhaps it would be Elisa's time to die.

"Here are the test results. Cubes seven, twenty, and twenty-three got the highest number of votes. However, the test subject in cube one committed suicide. As we stated in the beginning, if someone takes their life during a test, the test will end. Cube one has spared the lives of the other three."

A picture of Elijah appeared on one wall like a television screen. "Doctors diagnosed Elijah Jenkins, test subject one, at an early age with a sadistic personality disorder. He marks our first death in The Box."

The lights blinked out, bathing The Box in darkness. Elisa shrunk back into a corner and cried. This was not how she wanted her life to end. She wanted to die in a quick and peaceful way, but now she sat trapped in a room as a lab rat. It did not take long before she had given up on the idea that the cube represented her mind. Somehow her suicide attempt failed, followed by her kidnapping by these insane people.

Ten minutes passed before the lights brightened again. The pedestal and platter of food had vanished, being replaced by a hole in the center of the room. A small roll of toilet paper sat next to it.

"You may now go to the bathroom." Jacob announced.

"In *that* tiny hole?" Elisa asked, embarrassed by the situation. She had wondered when they would allow her to go pee, but she hadn't expected this. She had been holding her bladder for longer than she cared to admit and she wasn't about to urinate all over herself, or even in the corner of the cube. Elisa had already stood naked on a pile of clothing, this wasn't *that* much worse.

She did her business, and after another instruction from Jacob, placed the roll of toilet paper in the hole. She shrunk back to her favorite corner of the cube and cried again. Elisa couldn't remember the last time she had ever felt so exposed and violated.

Elisa had always been a good girl. When she was fourteen, her parents moved her from Great Britain to America to live with her aunt. She received good grades, cared for animals as a vet's assistant, and she tried to never break the law. The problem was that no matter how much good she tried to do, there was always a cloud of darkness enveloping her mind she couldn't seem to fight. With the government outlawing most drugs, she couldn't use any to help her. After many years of torment, she had given up and illegally bought pills to end her life.

What would my parents say? She often wondered. If they hadn't perished in a terrorist bombing, her life would be different today and she wouldn't need to ask herself that question. Now, with them gone, Elisa only wanted to join them and be at peace. Suicide still wasn't out of the question. She had the gun, and if it meant saving someone else's life, she didn't think she would hesitate to use it. However, she wouldn't know until the moment came.

****

Barry clutched the pistol in his right hand and paced around the cube. He waved it in the air several times, hoping to intimidate anyone who was watching. "How could they know," he muttered as he continued his quick pacing. "How could they know I killed someone? There's no way. There's no way!" With a scowl, he turned toward each corner of the ceiling. "How do you know?" he screamed. His voice echoed back at him. "How could you possibly know what I did?"

He placed the gun against his head and then lowered it. He pointed the weapon at a wall. "What happens if I try shooting the wall?" When he didn't get a response, he pulled the trigger. The gun clicked, but no bullet came out.

BoX

"The gun only works when pointed at flesh," Jacob Harding answered with a hint of enthusiasm in his voice. "I have to applaud you for being the first to try it."

Barry screamed in frustration and threw the gun to the opposite side of the room.

"Barry, I would suggest you use the bathroom before we take away the opportunity."

"Screw you!" Barry countered, but after a moment, he dropped his pants with reluctance and emptied himself.

"Superb," Jacob responded as though he had watched the whole thing.

"Pervert," Barry muttered.

The woman's voice replaced Jacob's as Barry covered himself once more with the horrible gray sweats.

"Now, having relieved yourselves, it's time for the third test." The lights shut off once more. Barry fumbled around in the darkness until he felt a wall and sat.

"Welcome to your isolation. You will have no light, no food or water, and no human interaction until the test is complete. The test ends when someone commits suicide. Good luck."

9: Test Three: Isolation: Boxer, Chuck, and Tristan

Time ticked away for two days as The Box's inhabitants waited for someone else to take their own life. It was a morbid test that left no room for everyone to succeed. Somebody would die, but even though there were moments when people would raise the pistol to their head, they would convince themselves that they could last a while longer.

The hole in the center of the cube had closed and several of the victims had chosen a corner of the room to do their business. The rain began on day three.

A drop landed on Boxer's head. "What the," a clap of thunder silenced the curse as water fell from the ceiling. Boxer was an older man of Asian descent though he grew up in America. The water was chilling, but refreshing. He opened his mouth and drank what he could. He stripped off his clothing and danced, letting the water run down his naked body and wash all the sweat away.

Boxer's muscles felt weak from the lack of food and water, but that didn't stop him. He relished being clean and ignored the peculiarity of rain indoors. Were the others experiencing this? He sure hoped so.

He collapsed to his knees and drank in more water until his stomach refused. Boxer turned over onto his back and lay sprawled out on the floor, letting the cool liquid pour over his fragile body. He didn't know why they had given him water, but he wouldn't look a gift horse in the mouth. He would just accept it for what it was; a refreshing present.

****

Chuck waited in the darkness of the cube, wondering when an announcer, either Jacob Harding or the woman, would speak to him. They knew *he* knew what was going on, and yet they still put him in the experiment and allowed him to talk with someone else. The information he had would only do him good if he were on the outside, not here.

The question of how these people found him on the train still baffled him and Chuck had done his best to retrace his steps. He had used a fake passport, wore a wig and mustache of a different color, and spoke with a southern twang. He was a very logical person and being found by these people wasn't logical.

"How did you find me?" He asked aloud though he didn't get a reply. He flinched when drops of water landed on his head. Within seconds, the heavens opened in his cube and the cold water soaked him. "So, you give us water to prolong our torture?" He called out with a weak laugh. "Perhaps these people are stronger than you believe."

"We will break them," Jacob's voice appeared over the intercom. "We will break *all* of them."

****

Lucas Heath

Another three days passed since the great rain. The water had washed all the cubes clean of bodily fluids and excrement before draining into holes that opened all over the floor. It had been almost a week without food, causing The Box's test subjects to sleep most of the time. Certain individuals sat naked in the dark and continued to wring out their clothing for droplets of water whenever thirst became unbearable. Others continued to wear their garments and their body heat evaporated the water.

Tristan, a young lawyer, sat fully clothed, just waiting for the inevitable. "Go kill yourself already," he muttered. He wasn't sure if his words were for himself or the other subjects. Everything felt weak and the pain in his stomach was becoming intolerable. He had the gun at his side and it was just tempting him to use it. How could he go on living like this?

Being a successful attorney at the young age of twenty-four, Tristan had lived in luxury. The food he ate surpassed the meals of most people in the country, giving him a sense of pride that he was better than everyone else. In the past two years, he had never known a day without the best food his personal chef could offer, which made people wonder how he never gained weight.

How could everyone else be surviving this long without food? He expected someone to take their life days ago. Was it days? He couldn't tell how much time had passed.

BoX

Tristan gave up, and it took a great amount of effort to lift the gun to his head and hold it steady. He couldn't continue on any longer.

As he was about to squeeze the trigger, the lights of the cube brightened, blinding him. He dropped the gun and covered his eyes.

"Subject seven has committed suicide. The test is now complete."

10: Clarity: Shelly, Marsha, and Tommy

Shelly sat against a wall, her face gaunt and pale. The lights turned on at the test's end, but it took awhile for her eyes to adjust. She didn't even want to think about the person who died.

"In the center of your cube is a bowl of soup. Eat up," Jacob Harding announced.

She saw the bowl and made her way toward it. It smelled amazing. She pulled her long, black hair away from her face and ate.

At least the creators of The Box were smart enough to know about the body. Coming off of a prolonged fast, needed careful consideration. It must start with soft food, to let the body adapt to eating again. Eating anything rough like bread could hurt the intestines or make it more likely for the individual to vomit.

It may not have been solid food, but the soup tasted wonderful and filled her stomach. As she finished, a woman's picture appeared on a wall. She was blonde and had pretty eyes, at least in Shelly's opinion.

"Laura Lake, test subject seven, was a medical doctor out of Salt Lake City, Utah. She has a husband, but no children. She marks our second death in The Box." The picture faded when the announcement ended.

BoX

Shelly tried forgetting about the face on the screen and fell back against the floor, stretching out her limbs. What were her students doing now? Who took her place? Did anyone believe in her abduction, or did they think she left? She was a good teacher, the best, or at least that's what she strived to be. She often had to prove her worth to others around her.

For most of her life, she had grown up being called ugly, though that was when she weighed two-hundred pounds. After a year of forcing herself to change, she weighed one hundred forty. Sure, she was proud of herself, but were others proud of her? Was she attractive, or was her beauty an illusion?

She pushed the thoughts aside and focused on what had recently transpired. Two challenges ago, Elijah had killed himself, saving Shelly. When the woman announced which test subjects had the highest votes, the lights in Shelly's cube reddened and the number *twenty* appeared on each wall. She knew her number now though she doubted it did her any good. Thinking about a man who gave up his life to save hers, and he didn't even know who she was, brought a tear to her eye.

A crazy thought surfaced. Perhaps Shelly was worth more than she believed.

****

Lucas Heath

Another day of loneliness passed after the latest challenge of isolation in the dark. Marsha had eaten the soups set out for her though her body still yearned for nutrition.

When she learned of Elijah's death, she had broken down in a fit of sobs. The one guy who listened to her life story had killed himself. How could he leave her like that? Now, she felt trapped with the memories of her nosey parents. She had nobody and doubted she would ever find anyone who could help her. She poured out her heart, soul, and life to Elijah, and now she would never see him again. The world wasn't fair, and neither was this horrible experiment.

With everything she had been through, Marsha felt astonishment she hadn't lost her mind already, though perhaps insanity wasn't an instant event, but happened little by little. How were the others fairing? Had anybody gone crazy yet? A small clip of music being played throughout the cube interrupted her thoughts.

"Welcome to round two!" Jacob Harding announced.

Round two? Marsha wondered. Did he consider this a game?

"You all have done well on the first three tests, but it's time we get serious. So far, we have left you in the dark, figuratively and literally. It's time to change things; it is time expose everyone."

BoX

****

Tommy sat listening to the announcement, letting his weak body rest. They had fed him three times since the last challenge, each meal a different soup, and each one more delicious than the last.

"It's time to change things; it is time expose everyone," Jacob said. "Once again, welcome to The Box."

Tommy stared in amazement as the floor, ceiling, and every wall surrounding him became transparent, revealing the other cubes and people. His cube was at the top, on an outside center position. He could see the perfect, blue sky above and the lush vegetation and field below him. A woman was in a corner cube to his right, and a man was to his left. Levi the police officer had the very center cube. Tommy could see that Levi was watching him with intensity, rather than looking anywhere else.

It was the person who Tommy saw next that made his blood run cold. The Box was now clear, allowing Tommy to see into the cube behind Levi. He had the urge to vomit. He fell to his butt and pressed himself against the window that viewed the field.

Levi saw Tommy's alarm and held out his hands, mouthing the words *'what's wrong?'* Unless the creators allowed it, they wouldn't be able to hear or talk with each other.

Lucas Heath

Tommy stared at the individual who hadn't yet noticed him and tears came to his eyes. It was his dad.

11: The Dial: Chuck and Diana

The tension was thick when Jacob Harding came over the intercom and announced round two of the experiment. How many rounds were there? Did each one get worse? Chuck believed they did. He jerked from surprise when the walls, floor, and ceiling of his cube became transparent, revealing The Box in its entirety. He stared in wonder at the surrounding cubes.

Behind him was Diana, a woman whom he had talked with earlier. To his right was an older, teenage male, and to his left was a middle-aged man. Straight in front of him was a young woman who seemed as perplexed as everyone else. His cube was in the center, on the second floor of The Box. Diagonal to his room, another blacked out cube. The room below the older teenager was also dark, preventing anyone from seeing the person, or body.

"This is only the beginning," Jacob announced with a muffled laugh. "We tested you in three areas. First, we tested your pride. Would you give up your dignity and strip naked before an unknown audience to save your feet? Second, we wished to see how many of you would put the life of another individual at risk to save yourselves. The last test showed us how long you would push yourself to survive when all hope seemed lost."

Jacob took a breath. "The following tests will be different. For now, we want you to meet each other."

Lucas Heath

Chuck watched as the floor in the center of his cube rose, turning into the white pedestal. The same thing happened in each cube.

He glanced at the cube above him, seeing a dark square where the pedestal rose. "This can't be," he muttered under his breath. "How can a pedestal rise up from a transparent floor when I can't see it from down here?" He shifted his gaze and watched as a hole appeared at the top of his pedestal and a strange dial slid through, taking its place in the center of the small platform.

The truth hit Chuck, and he smiled. "It's an illusion." He looked down at the ground and noticed the person below him staring at their dial. To Chuck, it looked as if there were only several inches of glass between each room, though he bet that it was just a trick. Maybe tunnels separated each cube. Perhaps each wall projected a video of the other cubes. They displayed images on the walls like a television why not a live feed? Jacob spoke again, interrupting Chuck's thoughts.

"The dial before you allows you to communicate with the surrounding cubes. It will only work on your current floor and in four directions, behind, in front, and to your sides. To communicate with an individual, you must point both dials toward each other. That way, you aren't forced to talk with someone you may dislike."

"I appreciate the courtesy," Chuck mocked.

"The next test will begin in two days. Continue eating the food provided and build up your strength. You will need it."

Chuck stared at the dial and frowned. Other cubes surrounded him so, no matter what, he would talk with someone. He twisted the dial's arrow to Diana and turned to face her. She was already waiting with a smile on her face.

"Hey, handsome," she greeted with a giggle.

Chuck felt a sudden heat in his cheeks. "Hello, Diana," he said and approached the wall. He sat down and she followed his lead.

"So, we should get to know each other. What do you want to talk about?" Chuck had known she was from New York from her dialect.

"We didn't have much time to talk before, but you were about to tell me what you were doing before being brought here."

She nodded. "Yeah," she paused and bit her lip. "Since I don't know if I'll live through these next few tests, I'm just going to be honest with you. I make my living as a prostitute."

Chuck nodded and forced a smile.

"I don't like my job. I hate it with a passion, though I could never get away from it, or from the guy who controlled me. The people who brought me here did me a favor." She breathed a sigh of relief. "That's my biggest secret. Not even my parents know. This will sound weird, but most of the guys who," she paused again, "use me, never even look at my face. It feels strange that *you* do."

"You don't have to worry. I will not judge you for that. And how could I *not* look at your face? You're beautiful."

"Thanks," she said with an anxious giggle.

In Chuck's eyes, Diana encompassed what he had said. She was shorter than he was, bordering on five-feet, six-inches tall. Her hair was jet-black and fell to her shoulders and she had stunning green eyes that pulled at his heart. She was gorgeous.

"So, what about you? Do you have anything you want to confess while you have the chance? I promise that it's good for the soul!" Diana said with a nervous laugh.

"I have a lot of secrets," Chuck admitted with a slight nod. "But I don't think I'm ready to expose them yet."

12: The Threat: Levi, Tommy, and Nick

Levi couldn't take his eyes off of the young boy and watched as Tommy tried hiding behind the pedestal. "You're so much like Clay," Levi whispered as a tear came to his eye.

"Who's Clay?" a soft, quiet voice spoke.

Levi looked over at his pedestal and noticed the dial was pointing toward Tommy's cube. Tommy's dial pointed at him. "Clay was my little brother. He died last year from heart failure."

There was a prolonged silence before Tommy responded. "I'm sorry."

"He was a good kid." Levi sat down, cross-legged. "He was about your age. I didn't have enough money to get him the surgery he needed."

"I thought cops got paid a lot," Tommy muttered.

"Not at all." Levi laughed. "We get paid enough to live, but that's about as far as it goes."

"And your brother died because of that?"

Levi nodded even though Tommy wasn't looking at him. "Yes. I tried everything to save him. I even sold drugs the police had confiscated back to drug dealers though *that* didn't even make me enough." He sighed. "Tommy, I'm not perfect, but I'm not a bad guy. I have spent my life trying to save kids like you from those who want to hurt you."

Tommy stared through the floor and out the wall of the cube below him. He could see the field as if there were no distortions from the glass. Could he trust this guy?

"You're trapped in this place by a mad man. Nothing you say can hurt you."

Tommy sighed and looked up at the sky. He wiped tears away from his cheeks. "The man in the cube behind you is my dad."

Levi rotated himself and glanced at the large man Tommy claimed was his father. He chatted with a girl in a corner of The Box. He weighed no less than two-hundred pounds, and from his build, it was all muscle. A visible scar stretched down his cheek, though his long, brown hair covered part of it. Levi turned back to the hidden young boy. "He looks frightening."

"Yeah," Tommy squeaked. "He hurts me. A lot."

"I figured as much," Levi admitted.

"I have to love him because he's my dad, but he gets angry a lot. He can't find out I'm here."

"I think keeping yourself hidden will be hard to do."

"I can try."

BoX

"What will you do if you escape The Box? Will you go back home?"

Tommy shrugged. "I suppose. It's not like I have anywhere else to go."

"And you won't go to the police?"

"No, I can't do that. Dad would kill me."

Levi sighed. "I doubt your father would kill you. Sure, some parents can be abusive, but they aren't always murderers."

"A couple months ago, I had to have surgery on my leg because dad stabbed me with a hunting knife."

"And the police didn't get involved?" Levi noticed that the level of his anger was building.

"No. Dad told them it was an accident, and mama agreed with him. The doctors didn't question it."

"Worthless pieces of ..."

"It's okay, though," Tommy said. "As long as I stay a good boy, he doesn't hurt me. I'm getting better."

Levi stood and spun around to the dial. He twisted it until the arrow was pointing at the large man's cube. He walked over to the wall and waved to get his attention.

Lucas Heath

The man turned to look at him, said something to the woman, and turned the knob. "What can I do for you?" His booming voice echoed in Levi's room. The stitching on the shirt showed Nick's name.

"Do you abuse your kid, Nick?" Levi spat out the question with as much venom as he could muster.

Taken aback by the question, a confused and fearful expression filled Nick's face. "What?" The fear faded and anger replaced it. "Who do you think you are, asking me something like that?" he demanded.

"I asked you a simple question. Do *you* abuse your child? Did you *stab* him with a hunting knife?" Before Nick responded, Levi continued. "You are nothing but worthless trash needing incineration. You belong here in this experiment. Who are *you* to abuse a child?"

Too stunned to change the dial, Nick's muscles froze in place.

"Here's my promise to you. If I get the opportunity, I will destroy you. You will *never* hurt another kid." Levi spun around and turned his dial so that the arrow was facing Tommy's cube once again. "Don't worry, kiddo," he said with a sad smile. "Your dad will never touch you again."

13: The Pact: Nick and Elisa

Elisa stared at the tattoo on her hand while she waited for Nick to change the dial back to her. Her dark brown skin seemed to have lightened a few shades though she wasn't sure how that was possible. She figured it was most likely a trick of the light. Now that The Box was transparent, sunlight poured through, bathing her in comforting warmth. The scenery beyond the walls had a soothing effect.

Nick was a handsome man, and even though he was in his early forties, his long, brown hair had yet to gray. With the amount of muscle on his body, Elisa bet he was a bodybuilder.

She looked up and saw Nick's hand moving toward the dial. After a short time he turned it.

"You seem shaken," Elisa said when he turned to face her, her British accent falling from her tongue. She wondered if that was the reason Nick liked her.

"People are *already* losing their minds in here. That man accused me of abusing my kid and threatened to take my life if he had the chance!"

"Good heavens!" Elisa gasped.

"I never wanted to do this, but I may have to kill him before he can kill me."

Lucas Heath

"Murder is never the answer," Elisa argued.

Nick nodded. "I understand that, but if he's trying to kill me, I should defend myself, right?"

"I don't know," she stammered.

"If you could have saved your parent's lives, would you?"

She nodded. "Of course!"

"What if it meant killing the terrorist before he planted the bomb that killed them?"

Elisa stumbled over herself for an answer though she wasn't sure if she believed her own words once spoken. "We should never use violence to stop violence. Just look at the planet's history. We have used violence to stop violence and our country paid the price! And so did the world!"

"So, we should just surrender and die? We don't have a right to survive?"

"Not if it means taking the life of another individual!"

"Who filled your head with such crap?"

A long pause ensued. "My parents," Elisa spoke, though it came out as a whisper.

"So you would rather watch me die in front of you?"

BoX

"How am I supposed to answer a question like that?" she blurted out.

"With a yes or no answer," he responded with a sigh. *Is this girl a natural blonde?* He wondered. "Is his life worth more than mine?"

"Is your life worth more than his?" she countered. "I don't even know the man! How can I judge something like that? I am in a corner cube and can't communicate with him!"

"He's crazy though!" Nick bellowed. His face turned red.

"Aren't we all? Who are *we* to judge another person's sanity?"

"I think I have a right to judge considering he threatened my life," he snapped.

"He may never get the chance! Perhaps these tests won't give him the opportunity." Elisa could feel her resolve weakening.

"And we don't know there *won't* be the opportunity either. It all goes back to the question I asked. Do you want to see me die in front of you?"

"No," she responded, knowing his logic surpassed her own.

"Then what will you do?" Nick waited for several minutes for an answer.

"If possible, I will help stop him," she responded. Only a short time ago she had tried committing suicide, and now she would take the life of another individual? Was this her? Could she be insane enough to do such a thing?

"And how will you stop him?"

She hesitated and inhaled. She let out a deep breath and nodded as if agreeing with the thoughts in her head. "I will kill him."

"Then this is our pact, correct? We will work together to do whatever it takes to survive this experiment, even if that means taking out other individuals. Do you agree?" A smile spread across Nick's face.

"Yes, this is our pact." She stared into his eyes and felt adrenalin flowing through her body. She thought back to her church days when they taught her the Ten Commandments. *'Thou shall not murder';* the thought passed through her mind. This wouldn't be murder though, would it? Even God had the Israelites kill countless people to take back their land. A small smile formed at her lips. No, this *wouldn't* be murder. She would defend a friend.

This was war.

14: Watchers

Two days passed for the test subjects as they got to know each other. Some made alliances though nobody knew if there would be any use for them. They continued to eat the food provided and most of their strength returned, preparing them for what would come next.

Jacob Harding sat in a roller desk chair, leaning backward, watching the conversations taking place throughout The Box. He had the fingertips of both hands pressed together in front of his mouth as he contemplated the next test. Every few minutes, he would run a hand through his greasy, brown hair.

"Ivan, what is the health status of Shelly? She seems weaker than the rest," he asked as he turned around to face a large computer in the back of the room. Buttons and lights flashed.

"Shelly's protein and calcium levels are lower than normal, but pose no health risk. She received eight sleeping hours last night, more than all the rest," Ivan responded. The voice sounded metallic and monotone, a feature that Jacob didn't enjoy, though at least the massive computer did the job. Jacob's son had developed Ivan, short for *Intelligent Virtual Analysis Network,* several years before, though it was only within the past year they had gotten it working.

Lucas Heath

"I know I've said it before, but this machine gives me the creeps," Barbra Jenkins muttered as she monitored the twenty-five active screens. She fidgeted with her black hair, making sure it stayed in the bun behind her head.

"I concur. Someday we can program a different voice pattern." Jacob turned back to face the screens and resumed his earlier position.

"Ivan, are the subjects ready for the next round of trials?" Barbra asked.

"I have recorded ten treaties and four issued threats. All are healthy and ready for the next test."

Jacob watched the screen displaying Nick's cube. He hadn't foreseen the situation between Nick and Levi escalating as fast as it did. Tommy revealed more about his life than expected.

Those were not the only oddities, however. The personal connection between Chuck and Diana was a surprise that not even Ivan had predicted, and Elijah's decision to give up his life had shocked everyone involved with the project.

"So, what's next?" Barbra asked with a slight smirk.

"I'm still not sure which test should begin round two. There's so much we could try. The data we are receiving is astounding, maybe more useful than the previous experiment."

BoX

"I disagree with *that* observation. Nothing we do here will ever be able to match what you did before your son ruined everything. It all helps though."

"We've tested their pride, self-sacrifice, and their self-preservation. I think it's time we move on to their memory." Jacob sighed when he saw an empty carton of cigarettes on the table at his side. "I need to get another pack."

"No, you don't," Barbra snapped. "You want to stay alive to see your dream come true, don't you? Those things are a lot worse than they used to be."

"I'll be fine."

"Ivan, if Jacob keeps smoking a pack of cigarettes a day, what is the probability of his death within the next five years?"

The lights on the machine flashed before it spoke. "There is an eighty-one percent chance he will die within the next five years."

"Yeah, yeah," Jacob said with an annoyed huff which ended in a coughing fit.

"So, are we good to go with the trial?"

Jacob nodded. He grabbed a glass of water by his side and took a swig. "Yes," he muttered when he could speak again. "Get the lab geeks ready. We begin in an hour."

15: Test Four: Memory: Shelly and Barry

Shelly yawned and leaned against the wall that separated her from Barry. She was waiting for her cube to become translucent once more. Once a day, The Box lost its transparency so that the test subjects could go to the bathroom in private. Why the creators were so accommodating was a mystery, but Shelly appreciated not having twenty-four other people watch while she relieved herself.

Ever since being given the dials, Barry and Shelly had connected, which pleased her, for she felt less alone. Teaching a bunch of kids and then correcting their work left her with no time to be around people.

She watched as the toilet hole in the floor closed and the dial withdrew into the pedestal. A moment later, a red button took the dial's place.

"Welcome to your fourth test," the announcer woman's voice echoed. "Today, we will test your memory. For the test, your cube will stay secluded from the others. When we begin, the four walls surrounding you will light up in a series of patterns. Your job is to touch each wall in the order they flash. When you finish, push the red button on the pedestal to confirm your answer. You get one minute to input your answer. Tapping the button twice will reset your choice, but will not repeat the pattern."

BoX

Shelly stared at the red button and a cold chill spread through her body. How much more would they put her though?

"There will be five patterns to remember. If you fail a pattern, we will remove the oxygen from your cube and you will suffocate. However, we have given you *one* way to save yourself if this happens. If you can complete the final patterns before running out of oxygen, then you will survive. Two failures will cause immediate termination. Good luck. Tap the button to begin."

Shelly's body shook as fear took control. She couldn't do this; she would die. Shelly reached out and tapped the button. The walls dimmed and Shelly watched as the flashes of the pattern filled the room.

"Front, right, left, back, right," she spoke aloud. She jogged over to each wall, touched them in the order she had seen them light up, and then pushed the button. An eerie, green light flickered through the room.

Shelly breathed a sigh of relief and waited for the next pattern.

"Front, right, left, back, right, front, left, right?" She froze in panic as the last wall dimmed and then swore under her breath. Shelly jogged over to the front wall and touched it before continuing the next four pieces of the pattern. She closed her eyes to think. What were the last three flashes?

Lucas Heath

The walls flared at sporadic intervals as the invisible timer counted down to her demise.

Tears came to Shelly's eyes as she fell to her knees in defeat. "I can't remember," she mumbled. She turned and stared at the gun several feet away. She couldn't use it and she never would. Maybe she could still finish the final three patterns before her air ran out.

The walls flashed a dark red as if declaring her answer wrong, and she heard a hissing sound coming from the pedestal. Either she would give the correct answers to the next patterns and survive, or she would suffocate.

She exhaled as she stood. "Maybe it would just be better to die."

****

Barry passed through each pattern with speed and ease. He had a mind for memorization, something his father never stopped pointing out to him. Being the son of a governor was difficult, and Barry hated it. Abandoning his roots, he moved to Manhattan, New York and became a waiter at one of the most prestigious restaurants in the country, but then moved to Buffalo to live with his girlfriend. He became the waiter of a small restaurant and had been working there before waking up in The Box.

The people running the experiment knew more about him than almost anyone, which was disturbing. "Perhaps the people in here weren't chosen at random like they told us," he muttered to himself as he finished the fourth pattern. The person running the test had changed things up and lit the walls with different colors instead of the normal white flashes.

Barry turned toward the wall at his right and wished he could look through it. He sighed and wondered how Shelly was doing. She was a nice young woman, and he hoped she could pass the tests. She didn't deserve this. Maybe he did, but she sure didn't.

The final pattern began. Ten flashes of blue, red, green, and yellow light filled the cube. Barry answered it with ease and pressed the button on the pedestal. The room flickered green, and the walls returned to normal.

He waited for two minutes before the woman spoke over the intercom. "Congratulations. You have passed the test. It is unfortunate, but five did not."

The walls, floor, and ceiling of Barry's cube became clear, revealing the rest of The Box. Shelly's cube remained black, as did four other cubes—a second one on his floor, two on the floor above him, and one at the top

Barry dropped his gaze to the floor that now looked upon the dirt. A tear fell from to his eye.

Shelly was dead.

16: Resurface: Blain

Blain waited for the next words to come out of the announcer's mouth. He folded his arms, and a scowl formed at his lips. Five people had died in the latest test. He didn't care so much about them, but he was being experimented on too and he hated it.

The walls grew brighter as the image of a short, stocky man with red hair appeared.

"Don Foote, test subject eight, worked as an engineer for a major technology company known as Helios. He has no friends or family."

The image switched to a young woman. Blain estimated her to be in her late twenties. She had long, dark hair and a cute smile.

"Shelly Dawn, test subject twenty, was a grade school and high school teacher out of Wichita, Kansas."

The image of a young man in his late teens replaced Shelly's.

"Corey Bruns, test subject thirteen, received jail time after being convicted of the rape of a minor. He fled from custody at an appeals hearing, never being found by the authorities."

Blain continued to watch as a man with darker skin appeared on the screen. "Parker Dent, test subject sixteen, was an inactive marine. He has a wife and two kids."

The image changed again.

"Tristan Beck, test subject four, was a dirty lawyer from Virginia. He spent his life defending criminals, who in return made him rich. Isn't it interesting how none of these subjects took their own life to save the lives of the others? Look at what selfishness can do."

The image faded, leaving Blain alone with his thoughts. There were only twenty people left and who knew how many more experiments there would be? He leaned against a wall and slid down until his butt hit the ground. He ran a hand through his short, matted, brown hair.

"Do you know what I've done?" he asked, though he didn't expect an answer. Perhaps that's why they had taken him. Blain was only twenty-five, but he had already committed such evil, unforgivable acts. He belonged here. Perhaps a lot of the others did too.

Blain closed his eyes and hummed. It was a curious little melody he had picked up though he couldn't remember from where—probably on his travels overseas.

The sudden jolt through his body felt like he had grabbed onto a live wire. The light that penetrated his eyelids seemed ethereal, and the next moment he stood in another room.

****

"Follow me, Mister Mark. We don't want you to get lost now." A short woman with black hair tied into a bun led the way. She hummed an odd little tune though Blain had to admit it was catchy. He followed her down several hallways and into an office.

"Sit down, please."

"What's your name again?" Blain asked as he sat in a comfortable chair in front of a large, oak desk.

"You may call me Barbra." Barbra reached into one of the desk drawers and removed a pile of paperwork. She set it in front of him. "Here is the contract we have everyone sign. You firmly acknowledge that you are a willing participant in these upcoming tests."

"And once the tests finish, I get a hundred-thousand dollars, right?"

Barbra nodded. "If you succeed, and if that's what you want!"

Blain glanced through the paperwork and signed his name.

"I'm so glad to have you on board!" She stood and held out her hand.

Blain followed her lead and shook it.

"Well, then let's get started!" She removed a strange device from one of the desk drawers. "I need to inject you with this. It's a sedative which will also erase the past twenty-four hours from your memory."

"But then I won't remember making this deal," he protested.

"True, but this is nonnegotiable. It's part of the experiment."

"Then never mind," Blain said as he grabbed the contract and tried ripping the paper. "I don't want to do this." Before he could react, a sharp pain flooded his neck, as if someone from behind had stabbed him with a needle. He collapsed.

"Next time, let's skip the part about them losing their memory," she said to the person now holding Blain. "I'll keep my deal," Barbra said as she stared into Blain's eyes. "If you complete the experiment, you get your money. If you don't, then you'll be dead."

Blain's vision faded. He opened his eyes and sat back in the cube. Was that a memory? The sudden understanding hit him. He had signed up for this! If he completed these tests, he would get the money promised. "And if I don't succeed ..." He shuddered and looked around his prison. Knowing a prize awaited him was the motivation he needed. He would come out on top. He would win!

17: IVAN

Barbra pushed the microphone away from her mouth as soon as she finished her announcement. "I'm surprised Ivan didn't predict *that* outcome," she said with a snigger and turned to face Jacob.

"Ivan is an analysis machine, not artificial intelligence. It only knows what we program into it."

Barbra rolled her eyes. "That's obvious, but he *has* been correct in his predictions."

Jacob sighed and coughed. He pulled a lit cigarette from his mouth and emptied his lungs. "My son made Ivan to help watch multiple experiments to give us breathing room. We need to finish his work and complete Ivan."

"And who is this estranged son of yours? You have yet to tell me much about him."

"We parted ways long ago over differences of opinions."

"So sad," Barbra mocked and rolled her eyes once more.

"Implant malfunction," Ivan's metallic voice sounded throughout the room. "The implant in subject ten, Blain Mark, has malfunctioned. He has regained his memory."

"Already?" Barbra snapped.

Lucas Heath

"Leave it to the terrorist to remember first," Jacob said and scowled. He dropped the cigarette into an ashtray and focused his gaze on the screen showing Blain's cube.

"Ivan, what is the likelihood that Blain will cause others to remember their contracts?" Barbra asked as she turned to the machine. Buttons flashed and beeped.

"The probability that Blain will cause others to remember their contract is eighty percent."

"The risk is too great. He could ruin the rest of the experiment." Jacob stood, almost knocking over his chair. "We need to finish Ivan. This experiment could be the last chance we have. We need to get rid of Blain!"

"What are we going to tell the others? That Blain committed suicide *after* my announcement?"

Jacob shook his head and glared at Barbra. He turned to the computer. "Ivan, with all the data you have, what do you suggest?"

The buttons flashed and beeped once more. "Recommend initiating final challenge. The probability of subject ten's demise is seventy-nine percent. The probability of subject ten failing any other test is less than ten percent. Changing the order of tests will not compromise the experiment."

Barbra's eyes widened, and she shook her head. "If we move to the final test, that will divide the population of The

BoX

Box in half!" she protested. "There are still twenty test subjects from whom we need to collect data!"

"We could always isolate him from the others," Jacob suggested as he returned to his seat.

"But that will throw the experiment into chaos. We need the same conditions for every person! Am I right, Ivan?"

"Barbra is correct," Ivan answered. "We must maintain sync to receive the correct data and avoid confusion."

"Ivan, is this the only way?" Jacob asked. He felt defeated. How could the implant break this soon?

"This choice has the highest chance for success."

"Fine," Jacob muttered. "Then let's begin."

"We need these people," Barbra argued.

"We will make do with what we have," Jacob responded as he typed commands into a computer. "By the end of this next test, we will cut ten more subjects."

18: Test Five: Sacrifice: Nick and Elisa

Nick sat against a wall of his cube, staring into space. He wasn't sure what to think, or if he even needed to think at all. His brain hurt from all the patterns he had to memorize from the previous test. He had failed one pattern toward the end, but succeeded on the final two before his air ran out.

The wall to his right faded, revealing Elisa in a fetal position on the floor. The other walls, floor, and ceiling remained opaque. Although the dial hadn't returned, Nick could hear Elisa's heavy breathing, as if she were having a panic attack. Perhaps the dial was no longer needed. He stood and walked over to her wall. He placed his hands against the invisible barrier and called out to her. "Elisa, are you okay?"

Startled, she looked up and shook her head.

"Take slow, deep breaths, honey. Slow, deep breaths. Do the best you can."

She took his advice, and after several minutes, her breathing calmed. "Thank you," she said.

"Did you lose some of your air?"

She shook her head. "No, but the fear of suffocating caused my body to believe it was happening. I'm blessed to have gotten through the test without dying from my brain." She sat up and leaned against the pedestal.

BoX

She sat in silence for a while as her breathing normalized. "Five people died," she said.

Nick nodded. "I know. I don't like it. How many more will go next?"

As if on cue, the lights in both cubes tinted yellow and flashed.

"Your next test has begun!" Jacob Harding announced.

"Another test, already?" Nick bellowed. "As if we haven't been through enough!"

"This challenge is much simpler than the last. We have isolated each one of you with another person. Your goal is to convince the other individual why they should sacrifice their life to save yours. The test subject who makes the choice to die will push the button on their pedestal. Their cube will fill with gas and the survivor will watch the life drain out of them. You have five minutes to decide. If neither of you has pushed the button by then, you both shall die. Oh, and one more thing. Taking your life with the gun will not end this test. Good luck! Your time begins now."

On the opaque walls, a countdown timer appeared and flashed.

"Aren't they moving things along rather fast?" Nick asked. He grimaced at the thought of what would come next.

Lucas Heath

"This had to happen at some point," Elisa mumbled. "It looks like the pact we made was useless. We decide each other's fate and not the fate of your enemy."

Her thick, British accent was clear, and Nick found it cute. He liked British chicks, especially black ones. Too bad she wouldn't be around much longer. "If this is happening to everyone, it will divide the cube's population in half," he said.

"So, which one of us will it be?" Elisa asked. She stood and stared at the large man on the other side of the glass wall.

"I will not manipulate you, because I know you are smart and can see through that," Nick said and included a sigh. "I'm just going to be honest. My son and my wife need me. I'm the one who provides for them and I'm sure you know how hard it is for women to get a fair job these days. My wife won't last long."

Elisa nodded. "I understand. Your family is important. I've spent a lot of time searching for my parents' killer, but without results, except for a name. I always blamed him for my depression."

"Not to sound crude, but you told me you tried taking your life before," Nick paused for a moment. "Perhaps it's time you end it. At least *this* time you're saving someone. You would save my family."

BoX

She nodded and turned her focus to the button. "Perhaps you're right. Maybe it's time to let go. I'll get to be with my parents again."

"You're an amazing woman. If you do this, my family and I will always remember you."

Elisa's eyebrows fell, and she forced a smile. She lifted her hand over the button. "Take care of your kid. Be the best father you can be." She slammed her hand down, and a hiss filled the room.

Nick watched as Elisa sat and leaned against the pedestal. She closed her eyes and inhaled. After a few minutes, he couldn't see her chest moving any longer and she slumped to her side. Her cube darkened and the countdown timer disappeared.

"Pathetic girl, so easily manipulated," he muttered. He sat and leaned against the now black wall. In a few short minutes, only ten people would remain. The tests would end soon, and he planned on succeeding at all of them.

19: Test Five: Sacrifice: Tommy and Levi

The announcement revealing the next challenge came as a shock to Tommy. Ignoring Levi's reassurances, he raced around his cube, kicking at the pedestal with his bare feet, punching at the walls, hoping to activate a secret door to free him. He picked up the gun and, pointing it at the wall, pulled the trigger. The gun didn't fire. He screamed and threw it at the barrier, yet made no mark.

"Tommy, calm down!" Levi pleaded.

Tommy turned to the man. "Calm down? You *seriously* want me to calm down?" he yelled, though his voice cracked. "Either I will die in this test or I'm stuck here with my father!"

"You don't know he will survive," Levi countered.

"He's Nick, the master of manipulation. He will survive!" Tommy picked up the gun and slammed the handle against the wall. "What the heck is this thing made from?"

"Tommy, please! We don't have much time left." Levi looked at the countdown on the wall. Three minutes remained.

Tommy turned to the police officer and scowled. "And how do you propose we decide who dies?" he snapped.

BoX

The venom in the boy's question surprised Levi. This was a side of Tommy he hadn't expected though he pushed past the surprise. Abused kids often had moments of rage and anger in stressful situations. "I would be lying if I said I wanted to die," he said.

"So, then tell me, oh great officer," Tommy mocked. "Which one of us will survive? Whoever lives will have to deal with my dad."

Levi rubbed his forehead and exhaled. What could he do in this situation? What *should* he do? He didn't want to die, but Tommy was just a young kid with the possibility of a bright future. However, that would only be possible if Tommy found a better family where his life wasn't in jeopardy. He had a fantastic mind, of that there was no doubt. According to Tommy, he had sailed through every pattern without a mistake.

If Levi survived, he could become a detective, devoting his life to helping and protecting youth. He could do a lot of good himself, and the chances of that happening were a lot higher. Sure, Tommy reminded him of his younger brother, but was he willing to take the chance that his death could be in vain? If both Tommy and Nick survived, Levi's death would be pointless. The decision was maddening and Levi felt the weight of it.

"You're not answering me," Tommy said; his voice was quieter now. "Which one of us will it be? Are we both going to die in this hell?" He pointed to the timer which now displayed that less than two minutes remained.

"There's so much good we both can do if we get out of here," Levi said.

"Yeah? What good do you think *I* could do?" Tommy asked.

Levi wasn't sure if the boy was mocking him, but he answered anyway. "I see a lot of potential in you to change the lives of others. You could help people who have been in similar situations as you."

"I'm too young for that," Tommy protested.

Levi nodded. "Oh, I know, but I'm talking about something that will happen later. If you use your amazing brain and work hard in school, and decide that you won't let anything get in your way, you could become great. The country is lacking in youth with ambition."

"Have you seen the crap going down these days?" the boy asked. "It doesn't help that our country split into four quadrants after the government reasserted itself."

"No, it doesn't," Levi agreed. "But that doesn't mean you should lack ambition."

Tommy shook his head. He walked over to the pedestal and looked down at the red button. "None of this matters if *he* survives."

BoX

"Yes, it does. Even if he makes it out of here, you can always get away. Find someone to help you. There *are* good police officers, you know. Some care."

"You could do a lot more to help people in the years it would take for me to become an adult."

"Tommy, no!" Levi cried out as the boy pressed his hand against the button.

Tommy kept the pressure down and gave a sad smile. "Levi, thank you for caring," a tear slid down his cheek. "I can see now that my dad is a liar. I should have seen it before, but I didn't. Just help people. That's all I want you to do for me. Just help people." He looked at the timer and saw thirty seconds remaining. He removed his hand from the button.

The look of confusion on Levi's face was clear as a hissing sound filled his cube. "What?" Levi mumbled as he turned toward his own pedestal. Tiny holes had appeared at the base.

The young boy ran to the wall leading to Levi's cube. "No!" He screamed. "I chose myself!" He pounded his fists against the barrier. "You stupid people, I chose to die, not him!" Tears streamed down Tommy's face as Levi's eyelids drooped. The older man collapsed to his knees and then to his side.

Lucas Heath

Tommy screamed the loudest he could. It was a cry of agony and guilt, of sorrow and sadness, of fear and shame. The countdown timer had turned off, and for a few short minutes, as Tommy pressed his hands against the wall, he watched Levi die. The police officer's cube went black.

20: Test Five: Sacrifice: Chuck and Diana

"You are the most amazing man I have ever met," Diana said with a giggle. She turned away to hide her blushing face.

Chuck smiled and sat back against the pedestal. "I don't think I would call a photographic memory amazing. It's a gift and a curse. Sometimes, there are images you don't want to remember."

She turned back to face him when she was sure the color of her cheeks had returned to normal. "Is it wrong that I enjoyed that last test?"

Chuck shrugged. "I don't think so. It's better than letting fear grip you and prevent you from succeeding."

She stared at him for several moments. "Who *are* you? Why were you brought in here?"

"That's a complicated question," Chuck replied with an intense frown.

"I don't believe they chose us to be here in The Box at random."

Chuck nodded. "You noticed that too? You are perceptive."

"So ... who are you? Why were you chosen? The teenager who had been in the cube next to you; they said he was a rapist. Then, there was that lawyer who helped criminals. I'm a prostitute. Have *you* done something wrong?"

Chuck sighed. "Yes, I have. Years ago, I tried killing my father."

She gasped and placed a hand over her mouth.

"He was insane, trying to achieve things that no man should. His death was the only logical course of action I could see."

"And that's why they brought you in here?" Diana lowered her head and stared at the ground. "That's a sad secret to hold."

Chuck nodded. "I won't deny that the guilt is strong sometimes."

The lights in both cubes tinted to the color cyan and flashed.

"Your next test has begun!" Jacob announced. "This challenge is much simpler than the last. We have isolated each one of you with another person. Your goal is to convince the other individual why they should sacrifice their life to save yours. The test subject who makes the choice to die will push the button on their pedestal. Their cube will fill with gas and the survivor will watch the life drain out of them. You have five minutes to decide. If neither of you has pushed the button by then, you both shall die. Oh, and one more thing. Taking your life with the gun will not end this test. Good luck! Your time begins now."

Chuck's eyes grew wide, and he shook his head. "Oh my ..." he didn't finish his sentence, but stood. He went for the pistol in the corner of the room. "I got my answer," he said as he grabbed the weapon and turned to a terrified Diana.

"What are you doing?" she stammered. She stood and placed her hands against the barrier that separated them.

Chuck turned and looked at the new timer displayed on his wall. He had four and a half minutes.

"One of us has to die," Diana stated as she turned to look at the button.

"Don't you even think about it," Chuck said as he held up his hand, palm out. "Dad!" he screamed at the top of his lungs as he looked up at the ceiling. "Dad! I know you're watching!"

"You're calling out to your father?" Diana asked. "I'm confused." She turned and stared at the captivating man.

Chuck focused on her, a twinkle in his eye. "My name is Charles Harding. My father is Jacob."

Diana froze. She stared at the man on the opposite side of the glass.

"Dad!" Chuck called again. "I told you I would stop you!" his lungs were already burning from the force of his screams. "You won't win!" He walked over to the button and smiled at Diana. "I will keep you safe," he said. He turned toward the ceiling one last time. "Ivan!" He screamed. "Activate initiative twelve!" With that final call, he slammed his hand down on the button.

Diana could see small holes opening on Chuck's pedestal, and a hissing sound filled his cube.

Chuck raised the gun to his head, his focus never breaking from her eyes. "Goodbye, Diana," he said, and then pulled the trigger. The gunshot echoed as Chuck's cube went black.

She fell backward in shock, landing hard on her bottom. "What just happened?" she asked aloud, hoping to come up with an answer that would reassure her. "What just happened?"

The event she had seen would stay a mystery, but there was one thing she knew for certain.

"I'm now alone."

21: Forgiveness: Blain

Blain huddled in the corner of his cube, holding his legs close to his body. Tears dripped down his cheeks as he cried harder than ever. He hated himself for being such a good manipulator. He could no longer handle being the reason people died. "I'm *not* evil," he whispered.

The man partnered with Blain was Kane Petterson, a young musician who dreamt of fame and fortune. However, his dream ended along with his life as Blain convinced him to push the button.

Blain wasn't sure how much time had passed, but the red color of the walls returned to the familiar pure white.

"Hello, subjects," an odd, metallic voice echoed through the cube. "My name is Ivan. I am sorry to report that we lost eleven subjects."

Blain waited and listened to the names of those who had died. Two subjects were married and neither of them had pushed the button, opting to die together. Another victim turned out to be the son of Jacob Harding. The names and pictures passed by without meaning until one familiar face appeared on the wall.

"Elisa Tyler, subject twenty-seven, was a young woman who spent most of her life searching for her parents' killer. She was from England, but moved to America at a young age."

Lucas Heath

Blain stared at the face on the screen and his blood ran cold. He missed hearing the rest of the names, for the image of Elisa's face burned upon his mind. "There's no way," he muttered as he felt the tears threatening to surge forth for another round of torment. He stood. "Did you guys set this up?" he screamed.

The strange voice who had been announcing the victims responded. "Please be more specific with your question."

"You guys put Elisa in here because of me, didn't you?"

"Your assumption is flawed," Ivan responded. "You assume that she is here because of you, when in reality, you are in here because of her."

****

"So, Elisa, tell me why you want to be part of our experiment." Barbra sat on the opposite side of a desk from the young woman. Her smile held a tender warmth.

Elisa shrugged, causing black, braided hair to slip from behind her shoulders and fall over her face. She pushed it back into place. "Someone told me that if I take part in this experiment, my payment would be anything I want; anything within reason."

Barbra nodded. "Then what would you like as your reward?"

BoX

Elisa sighed. "For a long time, I searched for the man who killed my parents. He was a well-known terrorist in Europe. I'm told he went by the name of Blain. I tried tracking him down, but I've given up hope. If I take part in this experiment, then I want you to find him for me so I can meet him."

"You should know we don't condone murder," Barbra informed.

Elisa shook her head. "I don't want to kill him. I want to talk with him. That's *all* I want."

Barbra removed a packet of papers from the desk drawer and placed it in front of Elisa. "By signing this contract, you acknowledge that you are a willing participant in these upcoming tests. In payment, you will get what you have asked. We will find this person."

Elisa looked it over and filled it out. She signed her name.

"Good!" Barbra removed a small device from another drawer. "Now, let's get started. I need to inject you with a sedative. It won't hurt, but it will erase the past twenty-four hours from your memory."

Elisa nodded. "If that's what it takes, then let's do this." She watched as Barbra placed the device against her skin and injected her. Within moments, she had fallen asleep.

Lucas Heath

"Take her back home." Barbra gave the command to a man who had entered the room. "We will take her again when the time comes. But for now, we need to find this man Blain."

****

"I'm here because of her?" Blain asked, mystified.

"Her prize for completing these trials was to get a moment to talk with you," Ivan responded.

"And yet that doesn't make sense. What if I died, and she succeeded? She wouldn't get her reward."

"Once again, you make a poor assumption. You assume that every single person in this experiment dies when they fail. Before the experiment began, she recorded a video for you in case she didn't succeed. I will play it now."

Blain watched as the image of Elisa appeared on a wall. He stood and walked over to it. The recording looked so lifelike as though she were standing several feet away from him.

Elisa sighed. "Hello, Blain," she said. It looked as though she were about to cry. "Since you are watching this, it means I have failed at completing the experiment. It is with great thanks they have allowed me to record this message and will give it to you. I doubt you have any idea what I'm talking about, and it doesn't matter. What matters is that I've wanted to talk with you, and this recording will have to do."

A tear slid down Blain's cheek. He wiped it away.

"Blain, you murdered my parents. Ten years ago, they died by an explosion in Paris."

He nodded, knowing well what she was saying.

"They were only a couple months away from joining me here in America. Their deaths ruined my life. Through intense searching, I found out you are the man responsible, and I tried to locate you. I wanted to make you pay for what you did."

"I was only fifteen," he murmured as a new wave of guilt washed over him.

"But then, I had an encounter with God. You probably think I'm psycho for saying something like that. It doesn't matter. He helped me through tough situations. Recently, I tried taking my life, but I see now it was a stupid decision. I have so life left to live." The sadness faded from her eyes and they seemed to smile. "I wanted to make you pay for so long, but that wasn't the right answer. Now, I want to tell you one thing, one simple thing."

"What's that?" he asked, forgetting for a moment he was watching a recording.

Elisa grinned and giggled. "I forgive you."

22: Shift

"Have you figured out what Charles did yet?" Jacob asked as he hovered over the shoulder of a technician.

The man shook his head. "No, sir, I haven't. I've been through Ivan's coding multiple times in the past and I don't understand what initiative twelve is. And now it's active and I'm shut out of Ivan's systems. I've tried bypassing the security codes, but they changed. He has taken over the experiment."

Jacob shook his head and uttered several curses. "How could this happen?" he screamed.

"Jacob, it's time you tell me what is going on here," Barbra said as she folded her arms. Her eyebrows furrowed, and she bit down on her lip while she waited for an answer.

"I'll talk about it later, but right now we need to figure out what Charles did."

"No, you will tell me right now!" she snapped. "Did you ever plan on telling me you placed your *son* in the experiment?"

"Not particularly," he replied and rolled his eyes.

"I heard rumors you forced him into your last experiment. I'm fearing those rumors are true. And now you forced him into this test too?"

BoX

"I did *not* force him into this test!" Jacob yelled, startling Barbra. "*He* put himself there, though now I'm seeing how much of a mistake it was."

"Then why keep it a secret?"

Jacob flung his hands in the air. "Why does it matter? The experiment is the experiment, no matter who is in it! You had no objections when *Elijah* wanted to take part!"

"Jacob," Barbra said with a calm voice. "I'm not saying it's a bad thing you let Charles be part of the experiment. My concern is that you kept it from me."

"It doesn't matter now, does it? Somehow, Charles figured out what we are doing with Ivan and activated a hidden command! Now, Ivan has complete control, which makes no sense considering he's only supposed to be an analysis network and not artificial intelligence!"

"Are you saying that our work has been in vain?"

Jacob shook his head and turned to the lab technician who was typing with furious strokes on the keyboard. "No, not at all," he replied. "The brain patterns and studies from the test subjects will still go toward advancing Ivan's systems. He *can't* be artificial intelligence. Charles is smart, but not *that* smart to program Ivan with that ability. Ivan has to be running another program created by Charles. We need to stop him before he ends this experiment."

"But is it possible to stop him?" Barbra asked.

Lucas Heath

"What do you think, son?" Jacob asked the technician.

The young man turned around to face Jacob. "If I'm being honest, I don't know, sir. I have the others working on it. The only logical course of action is unplugging Ivan from the main network and controlling the tests manually."

Jacob shook his head. "But then we wouldn't have Ivan's ability to watch the subjects, or to help with preparing the tests. We would fly blind."

The young man shrugged. "Sir, I would unplug Ivan. Since nine subjects remain, activate the shift. Don't do any tests for a while until we can get Ivan back up and running."

Jacob nodded. "I like that idea."

"Blain is still alive," Barbra informed. "What do you want to do with him?"

Jacob sighed and shook his head. "He has enough to ponder. Ivan just showed him Elisa's video. I doubt we will have to worry about him for a while. We will pair him with Kay. That will make for an interesting dynamic."

"What about Tommy? *He* pushed the button and yet the gas filled Levi's cube."

Jacob shrugged. "It looks as though Ivan took over and manipulated things to match his predictions. We can't worry about that now."

Barbra waited and stared at Jacob.

"What more do you want from me?" he asked.

"The truth," she answered with a sigh. "Is there anything else you're not telling me?"

The older man shook his head. "No, there's nothing."

"What did Charles want as his reward if he passed every test?"

Jacob shrugged. "Doesn't matter now, does it? He failed."

"I suppose," she answered, though she wasn't convinced.

"Brody, unplug Ivan and activate the shift."

The young technician nodded and stood. He hurried from the room.

"Anything else?" Jacob asked Barbra as he turned to face her once again.

Before she could respond, a young lady entered the room. "Sir, I received a report from Dennis. Chuck is missing."

"Missing?" Jacob asked. "What do you mean?"

Lucas Heath

"All I know is what Dennis told me," she stammered. "Dennis went into the cube to retrieve him and he wasn't there. Chuck has vanished."

23: Reunited: Tommy and Nick

Tommy cried long and hard, mournful sobs that shook his body. Tommy's hope had died along with Levi. His will to live; gone. He contemplated using the gun to end his life, for that would be the easy way out. That would be his way of escape. He kept the weapon on the opposite side of the cube to deter himself from using it. Even in the turmoil and sorrow, he knew he couldn't commit suicide, not after what had just happened. If someone took his life from him, he couldn't control that, but giving it up was another story.

He lay on the floor, curled into the fetal position. He never wanted to move from that spot. It was his place of comfort.

"You have come far," Jacob Harding announced. "Now it's time to change things up, yet again. Let's shift things around a bit."

With reluctance, Tommy looked up and watched as the opaque barriers around him became transparent, letting in sunlight. The whole Box was visible though most of the cubes no longer had people inside of them. He wiped snot from his nose and sat up to get a good look at his surroundings. The pedestal, along with its button of death, had disappeared.

Two people were still alive at the bottom floor, three on the middle floor, and four at the top. Tommy's father, Nick stood with his arms folded. He was two cubes away and stared through the glass floor at the people below him.

With the pedestal missing, there was nowhere for Tommy to hide.

Without warning, a blinding light flashed through The Box, causing Tommy to shield his eyes. When he lowered his arm, the change surprised him. He was still at the top of The Box, but sat in a corner cube. Every remaining victim of the experiment was now on his floor. Nick was in the cube next to Tommy with a confused expression on his face.

Tommy stood and watched as the floor clouded, hiding the now empty cubes below him. The walls in both his and Nick's cubes blurred and changed in color, isolating them from the others. Within a moment, they stood face to face, bathed in a blue light.

There was a look of shock on Nick's face when he saw Tommy, but then a sudden understanding replaced the confusion. "So, you're the little crap heap who told that guy I abuse you, huh?" Nick asked with a smirk.

"Dad ... I ..." Tommy began.

"Shut your worthless mouth," Nick ordered. "I don't know why you're in here, but until we get out, you will not speak any longer. Do you hear me?"

Tommy nodded when a sharp pain arched up his back and through his head, causing him to fall to his knees.

BoX

****

"Mister Starr, I have to admit your request is rather odd. We had no intention of including youth in this experiment."

"Well, now you will!" Mister Starr said with a confident laugh. "Someone told me this experiment is for a brain study. What better brain to study than one that belongs to a stupid teenager?"

"What do you think, Tommy?" Barbra leaned over her desk and looked at the young boy. She could see fear radiating from his eyes.

The boy shook his head.

"It doesn't matter what he thinks. I'm the father and I want him to be a part of the tests. Give me whatever I need to sign. Your man told me that if Tommy succeeds, I will get a reward of my choosing. Is that correct?"

"Yes, *if* he succeeds, then you would, but this test is difficult and the odds of him coming through it with success are low."

"Then put me in too and I can quadruple my odds."

"How do you figure?" Barbra asked as her brows furrowed.

"I'm worth at least four of him," Nick said, jabbing a thumb in Tommy's direction. "So, what do I have to sign?"

Lucas Heath

Barbra removed two small packets from a desk drawer and placed them in front of the large man. "What do you want as your reward if you succeed?"

"I can just imagine it now. Nick Starr, millionaire. If either Tommy or I succeed, then I want you to make me rich. It's as simple as that."

Barbra nodded and watched as Nick signed all the papers. "Superb," she said when he finished. "Then let's begin."

Nick jerked in surprise as a needle pierced the skin of his neck. He jumped up and spun around to see an older man holding a syringe. "What did you," he tried to say, but the rest of his speech slurred as the drug took effect. He tripped over himself and tumbled to the ground in a heap.

Tommy stared at his father in shock.

"Tommy, if you succeed, what would you like as a reward?" Barbra asked him, drawing his attention back to her.

"Freedom," he said as tears dripped down his cheeks. "I want a new family. I never want to see *him* again."

Barbra nodded and pushed a fresh contract toward him. "Sign your name here, and if you make it to the end, it will happen."

Tommy grabbed a pen and scribbled his name.

BoX

"I have to inject you with this," the older man said as he approached Tommy with a new syringe in hand.

Tommy nodded, closed his eyes, and waited.

****

Tommy opened his eyes and wiped away tears with the sleeve of his sweatshirt. He was kneeling down, clutching his head. The pain had dissipated though he now remembered everything. He stood and turned to the man on the opposite side of the barrier. "You put me in here?" He had never before felt so much anger burning inside of him. "*You* are the reason I'm in this place?" Tommy screamed.

"What are you talking about," Nick asked. The confused stare returned.

Tommy laughed through the rage. "*You* are one pathetic man? How that agency *ever* let you adopt me is a joke!"

"Hold your tongue," Nick snapped.

Tommy laughed even harder. "Or what?" he asked. "I will die in here, or I'll have a new family. It's a win-win situation. Either way, I'll never have to deal with you again!"

24: Closure: Boxer and Barry

Barry jerked, bewildered by the sudden shift in location. He had been at the bottom of The Box, and with a flash of light, he was standing at the top, staring at an older, Asian gentleman. Had they just teleported him? Was technology even capable of such a thing?

He turned around, taking in all the faces left in The Box. The floor, walls, and ceiling darkened an emerald green, blocking his view of the others.

"Hello, Barry. I was wondering when I would get to meet you," the older Asian man called out.

Barry turned to him. "So, they want me to talk with you, huh?"

The Asian shrugged. "My name is Boxer."

"That's a unique name." Barry walked close to the wall that separated them and sat.

"It's a nickname. I used to be a bouncer at a night club."

"You?" Barry's right eyebrow rose.

"You see me now as a fragile old man, but trust me. I was a lot different back in my day." Boxer paused and knelt down so he was eye level with Barry. "I have one question for you, Barry. Who died to get you to this spot?"

BoX

Barry froze at the question. "Which spot?"

"The one where you are sitting."

Barry shrugged. "I don't know," he admitted. "I think her name was Amy. She didn't talk much."

"Ah, and I'm sure you did all the talking to get her to push the button."

Barry's eyebrows furrowed, and he scowled. "Who are *you*, old man?" he replied as he jumped to his feet. "You don't know me! How do you know she didn't give her life to save mine?"

"We both know that's not how it happened."

"Even if that's not how it happened and I convinced her to push the button so I could live, who are *you* to judge me?" Barry yelled.

Boxer chuckled. "Ah, the ancient old query. Since the world began, mankind has used that question to make themselves feel better about what they do, while making others feel bad for noticing stupidity or expressing an opinion. Am I not allowed to have my own observations and opinions?"

"No ... I mean yes," Barry stammered. "But you are saying I did something you don't know I did. You're making assumptions and slandering my character without proof!"

"And what about the girl you killed back in Buffalo? Didn't the police have the proof to have you convicted?" Boxer's expression changed. His eyebrows furrowed, and a frown tugged at the corners of his mouth.

"How do you know about that?" Barry asked. His heart beat faster and blood rushed to his head. If it weren't for the green hue of the walls, he was sure his face would have been scarlet.

"Didn't your father, the governor, make the problem go away?"

Barry turned around and walked back to the center of his cube. "Who *are* you?" he asked.

"I followed your story. I'm that girl's *father*."

Barry spun around and his mouth hung open. "She told me you died."

"And that's why you murdered her?"

"But I didn't!" Barry protested. "It was an accident! I didn't mean for her to die!" Barry fell to his knees and the sobbing began. "Did the creators of this experiment put you in here to torment me? Don't they know how long I've been holding onto this guilt?"

Boxer never removed his gaze from Barry. His expression was cold and distant. "Then tell me, Barry

Franklin. What happened to my daughter? If we will die in here anyway, then at least give me closure."

Barry wept bitter tears as the memories of his past came flooding back to him. "What most people didn't understand," he spoke, "is that I wanted her to be my wife. I loved her more than you could ever know. I moved to Buffalo for her."

"Then *what* happened?" Boxer asked. Tears were forming in his eyes.

"The day she died, she was working a graveyard shift and wasn't supposed to be back until morning. I locked up and went to bed around midnight. She ended up getting sick, so her boss sent her home. I didn't know she had forgotten her key. Instead of knocking on the door and waking me up, she tried getting in through a window and knocked over a lamp. I woke up thinking a burglar was in the house and I grabbed my pistol," he paused and continued to weep. He buried his head in-between his legs.

He looked up when the crying had slowed. "I didn't even intend to shoot, but she appeared from behind a corner and I hastily pulled the trigger."

Tears were now streaming down Boxer's face. "And you didn't tell the police that?"

Barry nodded. "I did, but they didn't believe it. I was the son of a governor. It was a scandal that would make *them* famous. They didn't care about the truth."

Lucas Heath

"So it *was* an accident?"

Barry nodded. "Yes, sir. I loved her with all my heart. It truly was an accident."

25: Friend: Diana and Zirah

Diana sat in the corner of her cube, hugging her legs close to her. She cried off and on and ignored the announcement by Jacob Harding. She refused to acknowledge the shift in the cubes or that the walls had changed to a pale yellow. Maybe she fell asleep, or maybe she lost track of time, she wasn't sure, but the voice of an angel pulled her from the funk.

"You are my sunshine, my bright and sunny day. You're covered with the dew of night, but it evaporates away." The voice was pure, stunning, and almost hypnotic.

Diana lifted her head from her knees and looked at the changes to her cube. While all the other walls were yellow, the one she leaned against was clear. She rotated her body to get a better look. An older woman with graying hair danced around with grace, singing beautiful notes as if she had no worries or cares.

"How can you be so happy at a time like this?" Diana asked, holding back mournful tears.

The woman stopped and turned toward Diana. "Why *shouldn't* I be happy? I'm alive, aren't I?"

"What good is being alive when you're trapped and treated like an animal?"

Lucas Heath

"Oh, honey, that's *why* you should stay happy! What better way to show these lunatics they can't break you than to live as though you're free?"

"That's false logic."

The woman laughed. "Not at all! Freedom should be a mindset, not what is happening to you in this physical realm. You can be physically free, but not be free in your mind, which is the worst slavery. If you're free mentally, it shouldn't matter whether you're physically free or not. You can have true joy in the midst of messed up problems, which helps you get through them with ease."

"If only that were true," Diana said, followed by a sigh. "I'm Diana."

"I'm Zirah, and what I said *is* true! To overcome a situation, you have to have the mindset to do so."

"If you only knew where I've been, you wouldn't be saying such things," Diana said.

"Then tell me, young one. Where have you been?"

Diana took a breath. "When I was younger, I had a boyfriend who sold my body for cash and drugs. He threatened to kill me and my family if anyone found out. He later sold me to a pimp, and to keep my parents safe, I left them and disappeared. They don't know what happened to me. I can't get away from my life."

Zirah chuckled. "Oh, honey. You can either call it fate, divine intervention, or even coincidence, but I spend my life getting girls like you out of this situation."

"Really?" Diana asked as she fought back another round of tears.

"Really!" Zirah confirmed. "When we get out of here, notice I said *when,* not *if,* but *when* we get out of here, I must help you get back to your family and away from those nasty men." She walked up to the glass until she was as close to Diana as possible. "You're a striking young woman with gorgeous eyes. Your hair is also stunning. The man who marries you will be in awe of your beauty."

Diana blushed. "Thank you. There was one man who thought I was pretty, but he gave his life to save me."

Zirah's eyebrows rose. "Was it someone in here, or back in your other life?"

"In here," Diana answered. "His name was Chuck. He was kind and even continued to talk with me when he found out what I do for a living."

"Darlin, you don't do what you do for a living. You do it to live. To make a living means to support yourself so you can live. Those guys are keeping you alive to sell your body. You need to understand the difference. Like I said, it's all in the mindset."

"Then how do I change my mindset? How do I become as free as you are?"

"It takes time, practice, and most of all, patience. It begins with the decision you will no longer be somebody's play toy. You are a woman who deserves respect and dignity."

"If I did that, they would kill me."

"I'm not talking about standing up to your pimp. I'm talking about standing up to *yourself* and realizing that there's so much more to you than you believe. I've been where you've been, darlin. It comes with so much pain, and shame, and guilt. It will eat at you until the day you embrace the truth about who you are!"

"And who *am* I?" Diana asked. "You are correct when you say I have a lot of pain, shame, and guilt. I feel nasty, and abused, and thrown out. I don't think I could ever be loved the way I want to be. So tell me, Zirah. Who am I?"

Zirah smiled that warm smile and chuckled again. "You're worth it."

26: Partners: Blain and Kay

Blain sat cross-legged in the center of the room, lost in thought. The shift had come and gone and his cube glowed light purple. "How does someone just forgive something like that?" he asked. Elisa's message weighed upon his heart. How could she forgive him for her parents' death? Who did that?

He wasn't sure how much time had passed, but when he looked up, he saw that the wall in front of him was transparent. A young woman, who he estimated to be in her late twenties, sat cross-legged in the center of her cube, staring at him.

"I was wondering when you would snap out of it," she said. She had a southern twang to her voice.

"There's a lot on my mind," Blain responded.

"I wasn't sure if you had *lost* your mind and were in a catatonic state. I'm impressed with the resilience of everyone in here. I expected most of them to go crazy during the time of isolation."

"Well, if you think about the crap most people have to deal with in the real world, is this place so bad?"

The woman shrugged. "I suppose it depends on the lives of those trapped in here. I'm Kay."

"Blain," he responded. "I don't know what to think or feel at the moment. My life outside of these walls feels so distant."

"Tell me about it then."

"You mean tell you about my life?"

"Why not?" Kay shrugged. "It's not as if we have anything better to do in here, other than sit and talk."

"If you insist, but I'm willing to bet that you won't believe me."

"Try me."

"I was born in Russia, though my parents were from America. Times were hard, and when my parents were out of money, and we were starving, they sold me. I got traded twice, but then an anarchist group bought me. By the time I was fifteen, they had brainwashed me and trained me well. They had a problem with the French government and gave me my first job. I had to blow up important buildings for them." Blain paused.

Kay nodded, as if telling him to continue.

"I didn't know better. I did what they told me. They expected no one to die, but two individuals were there at the wrong time; a mother and father of a young girl who lived in America. I was so devastated by their deaths I searched for their daughter. I found her and kept tabs on her for the next seven years, but then she disappeared. It turns out she had been looking for me, to tell me she forgives me."

"Wow," Kay said.

"For the past ten years, I have been following my orders and I've hurt so many people who didn't deserve it. Multiple governments labeled me as an international terrorist over a year ago, and that's when I decided that I couldn't keep living like that. I couldn't stand what I was doing. The problem is, to leave, I have to buy my freedom. One hundred-thousand dollars is how much it will cost me. The creators of this experiment found me and told me they would pay off my debt if I made it to the end. It was that, or the group I was a part of would hunt me until they killed me."

"So, you put yourself in here to gain your freedom?"

Blain nodded.

"That's commendable and interesting. I hope you succeed. I myself have a very interesting life. With all the corruption in law enforcement and the judicial system, I took justice into my own hands."

"You're a vigilante?"

"Of sorts," she admitted. "You know the dirty lawyer Tristan Beck who died a couple tests ago? I spent a good amount of time eliminating his clients after he got them off of death row."

"I'm sure this sounds hypocritical coming from *me*, but what gives you the right to take the law into your own hands? When is it ever okay to use violence to stop violence? This is something I'm trying to understand."

"Why let convicted felons roam the streets and prey on the innocent? What if there had been somebody to stop you from blowing up those buildings? Those people wouldn't have died."

Blain nodded. "You're right."

"To be fair, I don't eliminate people outright. I'm not a savage or a murderer. However, I watch them, and when I see them go back to their evil ways, I eradicate them." She stood and stretched. "It seems you could be a useful ally. How about when we get out of here, you join me? Help me purge this land of immorality. Help me stop those who would prey on the innocent for their own selfish gain."

Minutes passed before Blain responded. "I suppose it would be a good way to redeem myself for everything I've done. Especially once I'm free from my debt." He stood and stamped his foot, trying to return the blood flow to his leg.

"Then you're in?"

Blain stared at the woman. She was skinny, had platinum blonde hair, a thin face, and even from the distance between them, he could see a flame in her eyes. "You don't look capable of hurting anyone," he said with a nervous chuckle.

She shrugged and approached him. "Looks can be deceiving. Are you in?"

Blain nodded. "Yes, I'm in."

She smiled and giggled. "It will be so great to have a partner!" she said.

"Let's hope we make it out of here."

"We will," she said with two nods. "I'm sure of it. We are fighters who won't lose. Now, when this experiment is over, this is what you need to do."

27: Freedom: Marsha

Marsha lay sprawled out on the floor. Her eyes were closed, and she tried her best not to think about all the people who had died in The Box. She was glad to be alive, but knowing how many others failed, broke her heart in a way she never thought possible.

Destiny Shock, a devout Hindu, had given her life to save Marsha on the latest challenge.

"How can I ever repay you?" Marsha had asked.

"Do good to those around you and live life to the fullest," Destiny answered before hitting the button.

Now, Marsha was alone, wondering when she would receive her freedom from the nightmare of The Box.

"Just let me go!" she whined. It had been a while since she had eaten and her stomach grumbled in complaint.

A hissing sound filled the cube, causing Marsha to sit up and turn toward the sound. The familiar pedestal rose from the ground with a glowing green button resting in the center. She stood and watched as the strange, white stand finished rising.

"If you want your freedom, push the button," a strange, computerized voice said. She had heard it once before when it announced the deaths from the last challenge. It called itself Ivan.

She waited in silence for several seconds. "Is this a trick?" she asked with hesitation.

"The experiment is complete. Push the button to claim your freedom."

She frowned and her eyebrows furrowed. She reached out and held her hand above the pedestal for several moments. "What will happen when I push it?"

"You will be free," Ivan responded.

"That's not reassuring," she said and rolled her eyes. She breathed in and dropped her hand onto the button. The white lights of the walls dimmed, and she watched a recorded video of herself.

****

"It's nice to meet you, Marsha. I've heard a lot about you," Barbra Jenkins said as she fumbled around in her desk drawer.

Marsha sat across from her, fiddling with her blouse. "I don't know what you've heard, but I hope it's all good."

"It is! I assume that your friend Brody gave you the scoop about the testing?"

Lucas Heath

Marsha nodded. "Yes, he did."

"Superb, then what would you like for successfully completing the experiment?"

"Land for my parents," she said. "I'm sure it sounds like a stupid prize, but my parents live in a city apartment. They've always wanted their own land, but could never afford it. I want them to live in peace on their own property, preferably out in the country somewhere, where they can relax and enjoy the time they have left on earth. I want them to have enough money to live in comfort. They've done so much for me, they deserve it."

"A noble prize," Barbra said with a warm smile. She placed a packet of papers in front of Marsha. "By signing this contract, you acknowledge that you are a willing participant in the upcoming experiment. If you succeed, you will receive what you've asked."

Marsha paused. "There's no way I will get hurt, right?"

Barbra shook her head. "Not at all, you will be fine."

Marsha signed her name at the bottom.

"I'm so glad to have you with us." Barbra removed a small device from the desk drawer. "I have to inject you with this before we continue."

Marsha nodded and waited. If she succeeded, it would be worth it.

BoX

The video ended and Marsha's mouth had fallen open in amazement. "I signed up for this?" Another hissing sound filled the room and a section of the wall in front of her slid open. She hesitated and walked over to the dark hole. She had to let her eyes adjust from the cube's brightness before stepping out into a dimly lit hallway.

"Please make your way to the end of the hall," Ivan instructed.

Marsha obeyed and began her journey down the strange corridor. It didn't take long for her to reach the end where a door led into a larger room. In the center of the room was a wooden stand with a briefcase on top.

"You will find your reward, a deed to land in Colorado and one hundred-thousand dollars, inside of the briefcase. Take it and keep walking. Do not look back."

Marsha grabbed the case and ran to the door on the opposite side of the room. She turned the handle, and with a push, the door swung open. Seeing what was outside, she stepped forward with confidence, into her freedom.

28: Return

"How in the bloody world did Ivan take over *again*?" Jacob screamed at Brody, the technician who typed with ferocious speed at Ivan's terminal.

"Sir, I don't understand it. He's unplugged from our main systems. It's not possible!"

"And yet it *is* possible! He released one of our test subjects!"

Barbra stood over by the screens, monitoring the final eight individuals. She grinned and made no attempt at hiding her smile. "Isn't this ironic?" she asked.

Jacob turned around and glared at her. "Ironic how?"

"We have spent so much time trying to turn Ivan into an artificial intelligence and it looks like your son already succeeded with that."

"Shut up, woman," Jacob said. "There's no way Ivan did this. Someone has hacked our systems."

"You're right. Someone *hacked* our systems. It was Ivan. Just admit that your son is smarter than you thought."

"I refuse."

"Well then, your denial shows who the ignorant father is."

BoX

"I would agree with that observation." The sudden voice caused Brody, Jacob, and Barbra to turn toward the control room door.

"Hello, dad, did you miss me?" Charles stood in the doorway, a strange pistol in hand. He pointed it at Brody and fired. A small dart hit the technician's shoulder and penetrated the lab coat. Within a moment, Brody slumped over the keyboard. "You'll find your entire security force is unconscious. It gives us time to talk."

"How did you find us?" Jacob asked.

"It was a pain in the rear, let me tell you. Initiative twelve activated Ivan's homing beacon *and* allowed me to get into the system."

"So you're the one who took control." Barbra said. "I told you, Jacob. He's smarter than you think."

"To clarify, Ivan was the one who took over, but I gave him commands along the way."

"Your father may forgo his curiosity, but I won't. How did you escape your cube?"

Charles shrugged. "When you began the last test to divide The Box in half, I realized that Ivan was the one who had selected it. I know my machine and how it thinks. Once I concluded that Ivan monitored my cube, the rest is history. Initiative twelve is a failsafe I built into Ivan to keep me protected at all costs. I knew if I screamed the word *dad* enough times, you would focus on me and so would Ivan. It gave me the perfect opportunity to activate the failsafe. You've always underestimated me, Jacob."

"Why haven't I been working with *you* this whole time?" Barbra asked with a chuckle.

Charles grinned. "I've known from the beginning that the gun wasn't real. I knew using it was my only way out, but I had to make sure that Diana didn't get gassed, so I hit the button. I didn't know what would occur after I pulled the trigger, but I had to take a calculated risk. It's amusing that the only thing it did was turn out the lights in my cube, as if the gun was only a light switch. I have to admit the sound of gunfire made me jump. Before the gas could knock me out, Ivan opened the door for me."

"So, what do you want, son? You have me at a disadvantage. Tell me what you want."

"Once again, you have thrown me into an experiment against my will."

"You are wrong, Charles." Jacob said. He sighed and coughed. "Barbra, find his recording. I named it Alpha Six."

Barbra turned toward the monitors and typed the name into a search bar. A moment later, the footage filled all thirty screens against the wall.

****

BoX

"Sir, we brought Charles in as you requested." A large man dressed in a black, security uniform entered an office with Charles following behind him.

Jacob sat behind a mahogany desk, sorting through papers. "You may leave," Jacob said.

"Are you sure?"

"I doubt Charles will try to kill me again. Is that right, son?"

Charles shrugged.

"You may leave," Jacob said again.

The officer walked out of the room and shut the door behind him.

"How did you find me?" Charles asked.

"We've been following you for months. Taking you from the train was the easiest way to bring you here, especially with how many people you surround yourself with these days."

"Why am I here? I don't want to have anything to do with you."

Jacob sighed. "I'm sure you heard about the new experiment I'm conducting."

Charles' right eyebrow rose. "You're running another one?"

"Well, after what happened at the last one, we need to catch up to Helios. With the technology they have, they could take over the country, if not the world."

Charles shook his head. "No, dad, only *you* would try something like that. You realize that two companies fighting against each other to advance their technology caused the third world war, right?"

"That's a myth."

"That's the truth and *you* know it! The technology war between Helios and Midas is no different. You need to stop this insanity! You don't want to help the world, you want to control it!"

"Control is what will get this country back on its feet."

"No, that's what freedom does. Control just limits people's creativity and prevents them from being who they are. I agree that laws need to exist, but your control is different."

"I was hoping you would help me with this experiment. You're the reason I'm doing it."

Charles grabbed the chair in front of the desk and pulled it back before sitting. "What are you doing?"

BoX

"I'm attempting to finish Ivan."

"What do you mean by that? Ivan is complete. He can monitor numerous things at once and record data while verbally responding to your questions. What more is there to do?"

"I want to make him into an artificial intelligence system."

Charles laughed. "And how do you plan on accomplishing that? Nobody in the history of this planet has ever achieved such a thing."

"The data we gained from the last experiment revolutionized our view of the human brain and how it works. We only need to conduct one more experiment, and once we receive the data, we can form a virtual brain which can learn, compute, and adapt."

"You're still insane." Charles stood and slammed his palms down upon the desk. "I will not help you with this and I doubt anyone else will. You would either have to kidnap people and force them to do what you want, or bribe them."

"We're going with the bribing aspect," Jacob said. "Before the test, we ask each individual what they want for a prize if they succeed. If they get through to the end, then the prize is theirs."

"And you will give them anything they want if they complete it?"

Jacob nodded. "We will give them anything within reason. We can't send someone to another planet or clone them. However, we can offer special services to help with their life."

"Then let me sign up for the experiment." Charles smirked.

"I thought you didn't want to be a part of this."

Charles shook his head. "I don't, but I have a prize in mind for once I succeed."

"Which is what?"

"If I get through your experiment, then for my reward, I want you to give up this madness and retire to a small island in the Bahamas somewhere, where you will never manipulate technology again. Is that a reward you would allow me to have?"

Jacob's eyebrows rose. "I would, but are you sure that's what you want? You don't even know how we are conducting the experiment." He reached into a desk drawer and removed a packet. He set it in front of Charles.

"Yes. I'm not worried. You've always underestimated me." Charles grabbed a pen and read through the contract. "So you guys use contracts now?" He signed the paper and shoved it back over to his father. "So, when does it start?"

BoX

"Right now," Jacob said as he stood. He held a small device in his hand. "Once I inject you with this, we will begin."

Charles nodded. "Good. The sooner I can get through this, the better it will be, for everyone."

29: Release

Charles stared at the screens and shook his head in disbelief. "You didn't tell me you would erase that part of my memory before the test began," he said.

"I recall you telling me you weren't worried about what the experiment was because I always underestimate you."

"Either way, you are done with this experiment. I'm ending it. There have been enough victims."

Jacob shook his head. "Charles, we hurt no one. Sure, they may be a little hungry, but that's not something a few days of warm food won't fix. You realize that nobody died, right? Before the experiment even began, Ivan predicted the nine remaining test subjects. He was correct on all accounts, except one. A girl named Marsha wasn't supposed to succeed, yet she did. Elijah Jenkins was the one Ivan predicted would make it to the end, and he was the first one to take himself out of the experiment."

"Elijah Jenkins, the teen I used to mentor?"

"He was the one who came up with the idea for The Box," Barbra interjected. "I have to admit, it's a clever idea. It's a fantastic way of bringing out people's true nature. I can't deny that I've seen amazing acts of sacrifice since this experiment began."

"And believe it or not, son, we *changed* people's lives for the better."

"I doubt that," Charles snapped.

"It's true," Barbra said with abundant enthusiasm as she pushed passed Jacob to see Charles better. "You have a prostitute who now has a way of being set free from her old life and an abused kid who will get a new family to take care of him. You have closure between an old man and his daughter's killer. Sure, the tests were cruel, but it revealed to people who they are deep down when they get pushed to the limit. It exposed the good *and* bad. That's what we were aiming for, Charles. That's what we needed to complete Ivan. We needed understanding of morals and decisions. That's why we had to erase the memories of those taking part. If they knew we wouldn't harm them, or that there were no consequences for their actions, we wouldn't have seen what we saw!"

"Barbra, be quiet," Jacob ordered. "Charles doesn't care about the good we do. He only likes pointing fingers at the negative."

"I want you to end the test and let everyone go free. I don't care about your data. I don't care about Ivan. Just set them free."

"Couldn't you have Ivan do that?" Jacob mocked.

"Ivan could only connect to your northwest hub to let the girl go. Only you can release the others."

Jacob walked over to the main computer terminal and input a command. "It will take time. The cubes are in different locations throughout the country. None of them are together."

"It doesn't matter how long it takes. I want them all released and free. And to those who made it to the end, keep your word and give them their prize."

Jacob nodded.

Charles waited and watched as a map of the country appeared on the screens, revealing each cube's location. "I have to admit, your technology is better than I gave you credit for, Jacob. There are twenty-seven separate cubes and yet all connect. Nobody would even think they were in different states from each other, especially with that line in the beginning about how everyone is in a giant facility." One by one, the red marks displaying the cubes turned green.

"Do you think we collected enough data?" Barbra asked.

Jacob shrugged. "We won't know until Ivan is back under our control." He turned to Charles. "Now, I did what you asked. Would you be so kind as to give Ivan back to us?"

Charles shook his head. "No. Ivan is *my* creation and I won't allow you to use him for your own selfish purposes."

BoX

"I had hoped, but I didn't think you would." Jacob reached underneath the computer table and removed a pistol from its hiding spot. He pointed it at Charles. "Your weapon only has tranquilizer darts. Mine has real bullets."

"You would take the life of your son?" Charles asked.

"Yes, I would, just like you tried taking the life of your father."

"Jacob, stop it! We aren't murderers!" Barbra snapped as she stepped in front of him, blocking his shot at Charles.

"It's not murder, Barbra. It's self-defense. He tried taking my life once before and almost succeeded. The bullet missed my heart by a centimeter. If I don't stop him now, he will continue to be a nuisance." He pushed her aside and resumed his aim.

"Father," Charles said in a mocking tone. "You are a murderer at heart. You don't care about others. You're the reason grandpa died. If you want to take my life too, then do it. However, before I came here, I programmed Ivan to initiate a self-delete protocol if I die. All of your work will be for nothing."

"You did, did you?" Jacob asked.

"Don't you love the irony? You're the one who gave me the implant to begin with, so that Ivan could monitor my health."

Lucas Heath

Without warning, a boom filled the control room and Charles fell backward.

A grimace of hatred and rage covered Jacob's face as he tossed the smoking gun onto the computer table. He walked over to the body of his son and stared into the vacant eyes. A bloody bullet hole was visible in Charles' forehead. "I don't need Ivan, son," Jacob said. "Sure, it will take a while to recreate what you've done, but I have *everything* I need." He turned back to a stunned Barbra.

"Let's go, Barbra. It's time to move on with the next step of the plan."

She looked down at the dead body and back at Jacob. "What about the experiment?"

"The experiment is complete. We've released everyone. I'll have someone take care of Charles' body. For now, it's time we move on to the next step. I believe we have enough data to continue."

Barbra nodded with hesitation. "Do you believe that was the best way to handle things?"

"I'm done second-guessing my decisions. I need to complete what I started. It's time for phase two."

"And what does that look like for us?"

"You'll see, my friend. You'll see."

30: Epilogue: One Year Later

It was late September. Tommy sat on a porch swing, enjoying a nice, cool breeze caressing his skin. He enjoyed his new life. Living in Minnesota suited him and he wasn't about to complain about the cold winters. The radio at his side shared the national news as he swung forward and backward.

"Millionaire Nick Starr has been charged today with the homicides of Martha and Tommy Starr. Representing him is defense attorney Tristan Beck, a man known for his ruthless tactics to win a client's case, guilty or not. With Beck's clients often murdered after winning a case, one can only wonder what a better outcome would be."

Tommy couldn't help but smile.

"In other news, Sparrow and Hawk, two infamous vigilantes with advanced technology and weaponry, struck again yesterday and stopped a bank robbery in progress, saving the lives of four bank staff and three customers. Two of the assumed bank robbers died on the way to the hospital, while the local police found the third, in a getaway vehicle, tied up and gagged."

Tommy turned off the radio and stood from his seat. He entered his home and smiled when he saw the woman who had become his new mom. "Hey, Barbra, is dinner almost ready?"

Lucas Heath

Barbra nodded. "It is. Go wash your hands."

Tommy made his way toward the bathroom.

Barbra sighed and looked at the calendar against the refrigerator. It had been a year since she disappeared with Tommy. Was Jacob looking for her? Maybe, but she couldn't deal with his methods. She had taken Tommy and ran, and there was no doubt in her mind they had found safety, at least for a while longer.

She had tried to keep track of the twenty-seven, though as the days passed by, she cared less and less.

Diana found Zirah, who helped her return to her family. They welcomed her with open arms and rallied around to protect her.

Marsha lived with her parents on their new property and took up a job as a nanny. She seemed to live a happy life, from what Barbra could see, anyway.

Elisa moved on with her life and got a job as a secretary at a small church in Texas.

Shelly's students welcomed her return, and that's where she continued to teach and work.

Barry stayed in contact with Boxer for six months until Boxer died of a sudden heart attack. Barry moved back to Manhattan, New York, where he worked as a waiter in a popular restaurant.

BoX

Barbra kept Tommy updated on the exploits of Levi. He had become a well-known detective who dedicated his life to stopping child abuse. As of two months ago, he acquired a warrant for the arrest of Tommy's adoptive father.

Barbra didn't care too much about the rest. Some went on with their normal lives while others tried something new. The experience of The Box had changed people's views and perceptions of life, including her own.

She walked over to a door which led into the basement. "Elijah, dinner is ready." Elijah had been Barbra's favorite patient and she couldn't deny that he was like a son to her. Before she disappeared, she feared for his safety. It took a lot of pleading and apologizing, but once Elijah regained the memory of why he took part in the experiment, he left with her and Tommy.

"Just a minute," Elijah called out.

Within a few minutes, Barbra, Elijah, and Tommy sat around a dining room table looking at a delicious meal: macaroni and cheese with hamburger.

She stared at the two young men before her and a small pang of fear gripped at her heart. It was an occasional occurrence, and she doubted it would ever stop happening.

Jacob had never revealed to her what the second part of his plan was though she assumed it had to do with recreating

Ivan. After witnessing the depths of his madness, the thought of him developing an artificial intelligence scared her.

"Barbra, you okay?" Tommy asked as he held out the wooden spoon toward her.

She snapped out of her thoughts and forced a smile. "Yes, honey. Everything is fine. Let's eat."

The End

About the Author

Author Lucas Heath was born and raised in the Puget Sound region of Washington State. From an early age, the fanciful worlds and characters he has created have found their way onto paper and with his developing skills, Lucas completed his first novel, Erased, at the age of 22. He sat on the manuscript for over a year before self-publishing it, after already having released the shorter sequel, BoX.

In writing, Lucas aims to be the epitome of a mischievous story teller, one who weaves tales of mystery and suspense, pulling readers deeper until they can't escape from his grasp.

You can read his blog and sign up for the mailing list to receive updates and discounts on future books by visiting the official website.

http://www.dreamwalkerbooks.com/

Or visit the official author Facebook page!
http://www.facebook.com/LucasHeathAuthor

Check out the preview of **Erased** on the following pages! Erased can be purchased on Amazon as a paperback or eBook.

Lucas Heath

On a quiet day in March, in the small, secluded town of Lion's Glade, a nightmare begins as the citizens awake to find themselves with their memories erased. Their past lives, as well as their identities no longer exist in thought, though a single word written in marker on their forearms and documents found in their homes give clues as to who they may be. Now the challenge arises to return things to normal and figure out what caused the memories to vanish in the first place. It's a race against the clock as the citizens try to discover the hidden clues that may lead to answers, hoping they have enough time to solve the mystery before their memories are once again, Erased!

PROLOGUE:

It was almost midnight, eleven forty-eight to be exact. The elderly man, needing to quicken his pace, disregarded his cane; he had little time to finish his task. He placed a folded piece of paper into a small, wooden chest, closed the lid, locked the clasp, and lifted the chest off the kitchen table. Carrying it to the basement steps, he descended into the eerie darkness as fast as he was physically able. As he reached the final stair, a dull pain arose in his lower back. His cane would have helped prevent that, but he didn't have time to use it; he was running out of time!

The man flicked on the light and hobbled over to a workbench. He moved it aside with ease, revealing a hole the size of the chest. He braced himself on a wooden stool, lowered to his knees, and slid the container through the opening. Out of a nervous habit, he ran a hand through his thick, white hair and stood. He set the workbench back into place, concealing the hole and its contents, and after turning off the light, preceded back up the stairs.

A groan escaped his lips as he sat down at the kitchen table, the wooden chair welcoming his tired back. He grabbed a permanent marker and pushed up the sleeve on his left arm. There was only one thing to remember. After a moment, he had the numbers 12, 21, 54 prominently displayed in black ink on his skin. The clock on the kitchen wall buzzed as the hour and minute hands met at the twelve.

Lucas Heath

A bright flash outside flooded through the window, filling the whole room and blinding him. The light faded, leaving the elderly man face down on the kitchen table.

AWAKENING

DAY ONE: CHAPTER ONE

Ashland; the band poster glued to the white ceiling was the first thing the boy saw when he opened his eyes. He stretched and yawned as he fumbled with removing the bed covers, then propped himself up with his elbows and looked around the room. A dim light peeking through the blinds lit the area, just enough for him to see. Newspaper clippings, band posters, and a small whiteboard calendar littered the navy blue walls. The bed was in the corner of the room, opposite the door. A lamp and digital clock flashing 7:02 sat on a dresser at the foot of the bed. Two sliding-mirrored doors covered half of a closet full of hanging shirts and a pile of dirty clothes.

Across the room was a desk with a computer and large speakers; papers covered the desk, and a backpack lay open on the floor with school books falling out.

He pivoted in bed and placed his bare feet onto the plush cream-colored carpet. With a little push, he stood and then stretched again. A wave of nausea washed over him and he bolted for the trashcan next to the desk, grabbed it, and heaved. Nothing.

"What in the world," the words escaped his lips as the feeling hit him again; it didn't last long, but it made his eyes water. He sat back from the trashcan and used the sleeve of his pajama shirt to wipe snot from his nose. Perhaps he had come down with the flu. He needed to tell his mom to call his teacher.

Anxiety struck at his heart as a realization hit him. He couldn't remember who his mom was. The boy bolted for the door and threw it open, charging down the hall and into the kitchen. "Mom!" he called out several times, but to no avail. Fear replaced anxiety as he realized that the memory of his mom wasn't the only memory evading him. He couldn't remember who his father was or even where he lived. All the details of his life, details he should know, were blank... even his identity. "I can't remember my name," he whispered.

A third wave of nausea overcame him, and the dry heaving started once more. Tears streamed down his face by the time it ended. With frantic speed, he looked around the kitchen, hoping to find clues. Perhaps he had gotten sick, and a virus erased his memories. No, he still remembered things... he was in high school, he had a mom and a dad... at least that was *something*. Oh, and he had recognized his bedroom and the kitchen! Everything seemed familiar to him, but familiarity was as far as it went.

A piece of paper on the granite counter caught his attention, and he raced for it.

Troy,

Erased

We headed out early for Detroit and I didn't want to wake you. Don't even think about having any parties. Mrs. Lyons will look out for you until we get back. Hope your date with Kelly goes well tonight.

P.S. There's one hundred dollars for random spending money in the cookie jar. See you in a week.

Love, Dad

Yes, his name was Troy, he remembered now, or did he? Was it a true memory? Or was he so far gone that he would take *any* name? Whatever the answer, he would stick with Troy for the time being. He looked at the clock above the stove and then stared at nothing in particular as he concentrated, trying to process his next steps. He needed to get to the hospital. It wasn't a normal thing for people to wake up without their memory, was it? He needed professional help.

Troy hurried back to his room and opened the closet. Rifling through the colored shirts, he settled on a gray one with the logo of a lion and yanked it from its hanger. Throwing it on the bed, he removed his nightshirt and added it to the pile of dirty clothes. He stared at his body in the mirrored closet door as if he were looking at himself for the first time. He had a thin face and light-brown hair that covered the tips of his ears and part of his forehead. Troy wasn't fat though his abs weren't visible – something he would have to work on later. He was at least five-feet, eight-inches tall, and even though his age remained a mystery, he estimated himself to be sixteen or seventeen – as there was not a hint of facial hair.

As he rotated his wrist, black writing scrawled across it caught his attention. He raised his arm to get a better look. *Troy18*, a simple message revealing his name and he hoped his age. Had he written it? The eight smeared a little, showing the ink wasn't permanent, maybe done by a washable marker.

Troy reached for the fresh shirt and pulled it over his head. He slipped off his pajama bottoms revealing gray boxers. He didn't have time to worry about changing *everything*. Pulling on a pair of loose denim jeans he found in the clothing pile, he looked around for anything that resembled a wallet. Why hadn't he thought of that in the beginning?

The search didn't last long. Troy found a leather wallet with a few dollars inside, but no identification. He ran back to the kitchen, found the money in the cookie jar, and stuck it in his wallet. Grabbing a pen, he scratched a line through his dad's message about the money and wrote to the side, *already took it,* in case he somehow forgot *that* detail.

Troy walked over to the front door, not bothering to check out any of the other rooms in the house. At the moment, he didn't care. He needed to find help and figure out what was happening.

Erased

Φ

Jessica Dailey, at least she assumed that was her name, stared at a paycheck on a mahogany dining room table. Her gaze hadn't fallen on the numbers, but at the unfamiliar name printed in black ink.

An hour earlier, a scream and gunshot out on the street had jarred her from her slumber. She ran outside before she was wide-awake and before her brain told her not to go running toward gunfire. A woman with long, black hair, wearing nothing but a nightgown, pointed a gun at the lifeless body of a man.

"When I woke up, he was in my bed," the unknown woman sobbed as her arms fell limp to her side. "I don't remember seeing him before in my life. I tried to get away, but he chased after me, insisting he must be my husband. He wouldn't leave me alone." She collapsed to her knees, and the gun clattered to the cement.

Jessica had run back into the house to call the police, grabbed the cordless phone on the entry table, and dialed the universal three-digit number. The phone rang several times.

"Thank you for calling the Alpine County police station. All of our circuits are busy right now. Please stay on the line and we will be with you as soon as we can."

Alpine County; that name was not familiar. Where was she? As she had hung up the phone, fear washed over her like a bucket of ice water. Looking around, she had caught her reflection in the entry hall mirror: blonde hair, blue eyes, a round face, thin nose, and full lips, perhaps mid-thirties, but she hadn't recognized the image peering back at her.

Then, at the moment of realization, she became oblivious to her surroundings as she at last embraced the truth; she had no memory of who she was or anything to do with her life! How can a life of memories vanish?

Jessica took a deliberate, deep breath and exhaled to push the fears away. It was not the time to freak out; it was a time to look for answers. Forgetting about the shooting outside, she had searched the house with precision and, having found a basket of mail, sifted through it.

Jessica Dailey was the name listed on every envelope; there were even several letters addressed to Mayor Dailey. Now, she stared at the paycheck and sighed. Her mind flashed back to the woman on the sidewalk next to the fallen body. The stranger had said she had woken up in bed with a man she couldn't remember. Was the woman a floozy, or had she lost her memory too and the poor woman had shot her husband?

Jessica walked back out her front door. The man's body still lay near the walkway to her house; the woman had fled with the gun. Jessica sighed again and stepped back inside her home. She *would* venture outside for answers, but if she was the mayor of Lion's Glade as her mail suggested, she would have to make herself presentable first.

Erased

Φ

Troy had taken several steps outside of the house before he realized that he had no clue where the hospital was. He turned around and stepped inside, in search of a phonebook. He didn't understand how he could remember objects, or how things worked, yet everything else escaped him. It was almost as if someone, or something, had targeted those specific memories and erased them.

He gave up the search and grabbed a phone. He would call the police and ask for help.

"Thank you for calling the Alpine County police station. All of our circuits are busy right now. Please stay on the line and we will be with you as soon as we can."

Troy waited for ten minutes before walking into his room and turning on the computer. Perhaps he could find the hospital's address there. The computer booted, but wouldn't connect to the internet like he had hoped.

"Blast it all!" Troy screamed and threw the phone against the wall. The impact didn't leave a dent though part of the phone casing shattered. He left his room and charged back outside into the sunlight. There weren't any clouds above him, just a vast blue sky. He walked down the sidewalk, not knowing where he was going. He stopped and looked at the house he was passing. Perhaps the people there could help him. He ran to the front door and slammed his fist against it several times.

Lucas Heath

After a few moments, the door opened a crack, and he saw an eye peek out. Troy could tell that it was a man because of a visible beard.

"Please, you have to help me. I need to get to the hospital, but I can't remember where it is. The police are too busy to answer my calls."

The man shook his head. "Sorry boy, I can't help you. I don't know where it's located. Something screwy is going on here." He shut the door without another word.

Troy kicked the door and turned back toward the sidewalk. "Thanks for nothing," he yelled and continued his journey down the road. He looked both ways before crossing the street when a new realization hit him – there were no cars. He had to do a double take and look at all the driveways he could see; not a single car in sight. He continued walking to an intersection. The view was the same; every driveway and street was empty!

If the one-eyed, bearded man hadn't answered the front door, Troy would have thought he was the only person left on the planet. That idea caused a new wave of fear to wash over him. He needed to find someone, *anyone*, who could tell him what was happening. A green two-story house caught his attention and a strange familiarity drew him down the sidewalk toward the front porch.

Erased

Before he even had time to knock, the door flew open. An older girl about his age stood at the entrance wearing a white tank top and jeans.

"Oh, thank God!" she yelled as she reached out to grab his arm. She yanked him into the house and shut the door. She dragged him past an ascending staircase, through an archway, and into a living room.

Troy thought it unusual that he didn't have an urge to pull away, but something about this girl brought him comfort. Perhaps it was her green eyes, or long brown hair, two things he liked in a woman. How he remembered that, he wasn't sure, but it brought him reassurance.

"Who are you and what's going on?" she demanded to know as she pushed him onto a leather couch. "Why can't I remember anything? Please don't tell me I'm dead and we're in Hell."

Troy shrugged. All panic and fear drained from his body. "Beats me, but I have the same problem. I was trying to find the hospital. Maybe they can help."

She shook her head. "I called the hospital and police, but nobody answered. Something *is* wrong. What is going on here? Did our country go to war in the middle of the night or something? Why can't I remember anything?"

Troy held up his hand to silence her and stood. "I know, well, I guess I don't know, as much as you do. I woke up with the same problem. It is doubtful a war would have caused this, but a terrorist act might have if it was biological warfare."

"None of this makes sense. I don't even know where my parents are. There is a note pinned to the refrigerator with emergency numbers while they're gone. I also found this." She pulled up the sleeve her arm, revealing the word *Anchor*, written in black ink.

Troy stared in disbelief. "That's *just* like mine! But different!" he pulled up his sleeve, revealing *Troy18*.

"Wait, *you're* Troy?" she gasped.

"I'm assuming so, based on all the clues."

"My name is Kelly. We know each other, or knew each other. I got a text message from my mom saying she hopes I have fun on my date tonight with Troy!"

Even with the seriousness of the situation, Troy laughed. "My parents also left me a note about our date. That's interesting. Even though I don't have a memory of you, you seem familiar. So does your house." He paused and his right eyebrow rose. "You said you received a text from your mom? Did you send one back?"

Kelly nodded. "I didn't want to tell her I couldn't remember her, but I sent a text saying something was wrong. I haven't received a reply yet."

Erased

"Well, for what it's worth, I'm here for you. We may not remember each other, but at least we found each other."

She nodded. "What do you think we should do? What if this crisis is happening to everyone else?"

Troy frowned. The possibility hadn't occurred to him. He remembered the man who answered the door said he didn't know where the hospital was. Could he have lost his memory too? "I think we need to start a journal."

"A journal?"

"If we lost our memories because of a virus or something, we don't know if this will happen again. We need to write everything that *has* happened, and *will* happen; starting from the moment we awoke."

Kelly nodded. "Good idea. There are notebooks on my bedroom floor I'm sure we could use."

"Once we write everything down, we can decide where to go from there. Perhaps we can get in contact with someone at the police station."

"That sounds great. I'm glad I'm not doing this alone." She smiled and walked over to the door that led to the front hallway. "Stay here. I'll go get the books."